CONTENDER

A TANNER NOVEL - BOOK 38

REMINGTON KANE

YEAR ZERO

INTRODUCTION

CONTENDER – A TANNER NOVEL – BOOK 38

As Tanner goes after a high-level target, the ruthless hit man, Soulless, seeks to kill the same man, leading to a confrontation between the two assassins.

ACKNOWLEDGMENTS

I write for you.

—Remington Kane

SOULLESS

THE ASSASSIN KNOWN AS SOULLESS WAS IN ARIZONA. Although he was in the high country and not the desert, the day was hot and the shirt he was wearing stuck to his skin.

He was using a telephoto lens to observe the property belonging to his latest target. Soulless had been given a contract to kill the leader of a drug empire that specialized in illegal pain medications. The target, a man named Franco Malone, had recently encroached upon the territory of a rival. That rival wanted Malone dead and had paid Soulless a quarter of a million dollars to make it happen.

Killing Malone would not be an easy task. Soulless had been surveilling the property for weeks as he looked for a weakness in Malone's security. The man was guarded by over a dozen men and lived in a secluded estate that was set on a hill. Along with the guards, there was extensive electronic surveillance equipment hidden throughout the forest surrounding the hilltop. Men with dogs also patrolled the terrain and the lone road leading to the estate was guarded and barricaded.

A sniper rifle would be useless given the distance and any attempt to infiltrate the compound would have a dismal chance of being successful. Getting near enough to Franco Malone to kill him was a suicide mission.

There had been an earlier attempt on Malone's life a week prior to Soulless getting the contract. One of Malone's own men had sought to kill him in order to take over the organization. In truth, the man was a spy working for his rival. It was his job to report on Malone's organization. When the spy learned that his real employer was willing to pay a small fortune to have Malone killed, he decided to do the job himself.

Being a trusted insider, the man had thought Malone would be easy to kill. He had made it into Malone's bedroom well after midnight while expecting to find his prey asleep and ripe for a bullet to the head. Instead, Malone had been alerted to his approach by a hidden and silent alarm system only he knew about. Franco Malone had slipped out of his bed and come up behind the man after he'd entered the room. Although armed, Malone had beaten the man into submission instead of shooting him. He had used his fists to accomplish the act. Afterward, an interrogation revealed that the man was a spy and that a contract had been placed on Malone.

Malone had been a brawler in his earlier years and was still fit and muscular at forty-nine. At six-foot-two, he was not a small man and had never been shy about using violence. After becoming aware that there was a contract placed on him, he had beefed up his security. His men knew that they would be given a hefty bonus if they killed or captured an assassin. They were eager to thwart any attempt on their boss's life.

Along with the guards, there was also a staff of three maids, a handyman, two groundskeepers, and a cook and her helper. The staff was allowed the weekends off and traveled back and forth on a jet that was kept in a hangar at the nearby airfield. The guards were also given time off at regular intervals, although leave had been placed on hold until the threat against Malone's life was ended. That gave the guards even more incentive to stop any assassins foolish enough to challenge them.

As for the regular staff, they still had the

weekends off. Upon their return to Malone's estate, they were all searched for weapons and they never had direct contact with Malone. One group of individuals did have direct and intimate contact with Malone. They were prostitutes. Malone flew one in from a stable of high-priced call girls on Sunday evening and used each woman for the week. Occasionally, he would request that the woman stay for two weeks, but that was rare. If anything, he instructed the pimp running the women to find new girls often, as he liked variety.

Soulless watched as the jet taxied down the runway and took off. It was Friday evening and the staff, and the call girl, were headed back to Phoenix. Soulless packed away his camera and decided to make Phoenix his destination as well. He had come up with a plan, had been working on it, and was ready to make moves that would result in Franco Malone's death.

MALONE'S COOK WAS A WOMAN NAMED MARIE Valente. She made the Creole food that Malone had grown up eating in New Orleans. Marie didn't know what Malone did for a living, but she was certain it wasn't legal. If he was legit, the man wouldn't need a small army to keep him safe. What Marie did know was that Franco Malone paid better than anyone else she had ever worked for. If he was mobbed up or some other kind of criminal, she didn't care. The man paid well and loved her cooking.

Marie's helper was her daughter, Heather. Heather was a dark-haired, blue-eyed beauty who hated being cooped up all week inside Malone's compound. The guards had been told that she was off-limits, as there was to be no fraternization between the security force and the general staff. That rule was hard on Heather as well as several of the younger guards. When the weekends arrived, the young woman was more than ready to party.

A week earlier, after stopping home following their departure from the airport, Marie and Heather had gone out to have dinner. Because she cooked for dozens all week, Marie liked to eat out at one of the best restaurants in their area on her first night off. That evening, Heather had met a young man who had sent drinks over to their table. At first, Marie had hoped that the man was interested in her and not her daughter.

Marie had given birth to Heather when she was only eighteen. She had often been mistaken for Heather's older sister when Heather was a girl. Now that Heather was twenty and Marie was in her late thirties, it happened less often. However, Marie had kept her looks and maintained her figure. The handsome man who had sent the drinks was someone she wouldn't have minded spending time with.

His age was somewhere between that of Marie and Heather, but closer to that of Marie. When he showed interest in Heather, Marie was disappointed but not surprised. After all, most men preferred their women young.

Marie had left the restaurant alone that night while Heather stayed and had drinks at the bar with the man, who said his name was Kyle. He didn't look like a Kyle to Marie.

Heather had arrived back home at noon the next day with a huge smile on her face. Later that night, she had gone out with Kyle again.

KYLE'S REAL NAME WAS SOMETHING HE'D LEFT IN HIS past. These days, he was called Soulless. Soulless had seduced Heather as part of his plan to kill Franco Malone. Had Heather resisted his advances, Soulless would have attempted to attract her mother, Marie, instead. All that mattered was that he gain the trust of one of the women and be able to use that trust against them.

Other than finding her to be attractive and an acceptable sexual partner, Soulless had no feelings toward Heather. She was a pawn in his plan to kill Malone. Her life meant less than nothing to him, as did the lives of most others.

After having dinner with her mother on Friday evening, Heather had spent the weekend with Soulless. He told her he was a salesman for a luggage company and that he would soon be moving to her city permanently to take a position as a regional sales manager. In the meantime, he was staying at a motel. Heather never doubted his story, as Soulless was a convincing liar. He had learned deception at a young age and was skilled at mimicking emotions and interest in others when needed. For her part, young Heather was falling in love. She had no idea that Soulless intended to kill her. Her death was an integral part of his plan, and so she had to die.

Even if his plans changed, Soulless would have to kill her. Heather could identify him. Soulless always killed anyone who could identify him. The authorities might obtain his prints or DNA from the site of a hit, but they had never gotten a description of him. If he even suspected that someone might talk to the police about him, he made certain to eliminate the threat. To gaze on Soulless was to die.

HEATHER LEFT SOULLESS'S BED ON SUNDAY MORNING and walked into the motel room's bathroom to shower. She was going to meet her mother at home then travel to the airport in the early evening to board the jet that would take them back to Malone's retreat in the mountains of Arizona.

Soulless had given Heather a gift to take home. It was a complete set of new luggage. The bags she had been using were worn and frayed, having been hand-me-downs from her mother. Heather was delighted by the expensive leather bags and told Soulless that he must have spent too much on them. He reminded her that he received the luggage at little cost because of his job as a salesman for the company he worked for. Of course, it was all lies. Soulless had paid for the luggage in cash. Before gifting them to Heather, he had made an alteration to the bags. Beneath their silk linings was a thin layer of a powerful plastic explosive along with slim electronic detonators.

Before leaving his hotel room, Heather remarked that she was going home to pack her new bags for the trip to Malone's estate. She asked Soulless if he would miss her while she was gone for the week. He assured her that he would and gave her one last kiss. He would not miss her any more than a carpenter would yearn for a board he had used to build a bookcase. Heather was a tool, an instrument, a

8

means to an end. Soulless used her and was incapable of feeling empathy for Heather or anyone else. All that mattered to him was the fulfilling of the contract on Malone.

FRANCO MALONE'S ESTATE HAD ONLY ONE ROAD leading in and out of it. To access the home, one had to make it past a locked security gate. The driveway stretched on for over a mile and met up with a county road.

The recent annexation of the road with a highway had increased traffic in the area. Drivers routinely left the highway and proceeded to move with haste along the county road. By the time they saw the sign telling them that the speed limit along the rural road was significantly less than that of the highway, the traffic cop assigned to the area was already on their tail. The local township was making a tidy sum from issuing speeding tickets. One of the cops writing them had his own racket going. He was on the take for Franco Malone.

THE OFFICER'S NAME WAS IVAN VINCENT. IVAN LOVED writing speeding tickets. He basked in the small measure of power it gave him. If he was in a good mood and pulled over a driver who didn't give him any crap, he'd offer to write them a ticket for a minor offense, like failure to wear a seatbelt. On days when he was pissed off at the world, he'd add ten miles onto the true speed his victim had been traveling. If they were stupid enough to protest, he'd pile on more tickets.

One time, with a particularly abrasive and indignant driver, he called for backup and accused the man of making threats toward him. That man spent two days in jail and had to shell out money to have his car released from the impound lot. The guy had failed to give Ivan the respect he thought he deserved and had called him a liar. Ivan was a liar; he was also wearing a badge and a uniform. Ivan thought the man should have respected the uniform and recognized that it signified that Ivan was his better. The county road he patrolled on the overnight shift was Ivan's domain; he wouldn't stand for being disrespected by a civilian.

Now, as for women, if they were young and good-looking, Ivan talked them up while hoping to get their phone numbers. He'd been on several dates with women he'd let slide on speeding charges. The ones who had given him cold stares had been issued tickets and sent on their way. On those occasions, Ivan soothed the rejection by uttering the word "Dyke" as he walked away from the women.

Most women were pleasant to him. He wasn't a bad looking guy, filled out his uniform well, and rode a shiny police motorcycle that was a beast of a machine. The motorcycle boots he wore added several inches to his five-foot, eight-inch height and he fancied that his gun turned on some women.

Ivan liked to think of himself as a modern knight. In reality, he was a jerk who became a cop in order to gain a small degree of power over others. While wearing his uniform and carrying a weapon, he felt less inadequate. Ivan had been picked on all through school and during his time in the army. Becoming a cop had changed that.

When one of Franco Malone's people approached him a year earlier, Ivan had agreed to take money to be a sort of lookout for the man. His nighttime patrol of the county road placed him in a perfect position to keep an eye on the side road leading to Malone's compound. If he saw anyone loitering around the gate, he was to make a call while letting his presence be known.

So far, Ivan had only scared off a family of out of state tourists that had gotten lost and wound up at the gate. The thousand dollars a month Malone paid him was easy money; at least, it had been. That was about to change.

IVAN HAD JUST BEGUN WHAT WAS TO BE A TWELVE-hour shift. He huffed with surprise when the gray panel van went speeding past him doing over eighty. The limit on the section of county road was only thirty miles an hour.

He grinned. He was going to enjoy ripping the driver a new asshole before writing him a ticket, and oh how he hoped the guy was stupid enough to give him some shit too.

The driver of the van ignored the siren for so long that Ivan was about to call for backup when the van finally slowed. Instead of pulling over, the driver made a right down a road that was more dirt than pavement and literally led to nowhere. The driveway had once ended at a home that had burned down in a fire before Ivan was born. Vegetation had reclaimed the land and the asphalt had deteriorated from weeds sprouting amid cracks. What was once a smooth black surface was a patchwork of crumbling asphalt and dirt. Ivan bounced along the uneven surface on his bike as he followed the slowing van.

By the time the vehicle had come to a halt, Ivan was seething. The asshole in the van was going to learn that he had screwed with the wrong cop.

Ivan was shouting as he dismounted his motorcycle a few yards behind the van. He was already gripping his weapon, although it was still holstered. He had failed to notice that because of the way the cracked and weedy lane curved and dipped that they were out of sight of the roadway.

"Driver! Step out of the vehicle with your hands in the air."

Nothing happened. Ivan took several steps closer and tried to get a look at the driver. From where he stood, the driver's seat appeared to be empty. It made him wonder if the guy was leaning over to grab a gun from the glove box.

The back door on the van exploded outward to reveal Soulless; the assassin was holding a taser. Ivan's gun cleared his holster just as twin barbs from the taser embedded themselves in Ivan's right cheek. Ivan screamed in pain before collapsing to the ground and dropping his weapon. Soulless hopped out of the van. As he approached Ivan, the cop attempted to speak but was only able to groan as he twitched from the effects of the electric blast he'd taken. Soulless freed the baton Ivan carried on his utility belt and used it to beat Ivan senseless.

SOULLESS LOOKED AROUND WHILE LISTENING. NO ONE had witnessed the attack and the hum of the traffic out on the roadway was intermittent on an early

Sunday evening. Soulless checked his watch and saw that time was growing short. The private jet ferrying Heather, her mother, Marie, and the other staff of Malone's retreat would be arriving soon. After stripping Ivan of his uniform jacket, goggles, and motorcycle helmet, Soulless strapped on the cop's duty belt and shoulder mike. The pants and boots he wore were already a match for those worn by Ivan.

Before leaving the scene, Soulless used a knife to slice open Ivan's throat. The cop had seen his face and could identify him. While committing the murder, Soulless was careful to avoid getting blood on himself. After checking the sky for the jet again, Soulless strapped on a small backpack that contained items he would need. He mounted Ivan's motorcycle and sped off to the hill where he had observed Malone's compound. On three previous occasions, Malone's private jet had approached the landing strip while soaring near the hill, flying over the compound, and circling back to land. Soulless was counting on the pilot repeating that pattern.

A GLITTERING SPECK APPEARED IN THE SOUTHERN SKY nine minutes later. A moment earlier a request had come over the radio for Ivan to respond and give his status. Soulless ignored the plea and concentrated on the task at hand.

Soulless was able to identify the object in the sky as Malone's jet. He held a small black box in his gloved left hand. The box had a red button built into it that was protected by a plastic cover. When the button was pressed, a signal would be sent to the detonators hidden inside Heather's luggage. In order for it to work, the pilot would have to fly the jet within range of the hill.

Soulless had seen him do so on two of the three previous occasions that he had watched the aircraft land. On the other attempt, the jet had been much higher and out of range of the detonator signal. If that were the case again, Soulless would need to improvise. Regardless of what happened, he was ready to fulfill the contract on Franco Malone.

Soulless watched with an expressionless face as the jet came closer. Not only was it on track to fly within range of the hill but looked as if it would be travelling at a perfect angle as it flew past. Soulless flipped up the plastic cover on the trigger box and placed his thumb on the red button. As the jet whizzed by, he pressed hard on the button. Nothing happened, so he released it and pressed again. Although he was unable to hear the sound of the explosion over the roar of the jet's engines, Soulless was pleased to see fire erupt in the belly of the aircraft. For several moments the jet continued on while its wings wobbled, but then the small reservoir fuel tank located under the cabin floor exploded, turning the jet into a hurtling fireball that weighed several tons.

Soulless watched with satisfaction as the jet lost altitude and headed directly for Malone's home, just as he had planned.

The blazing metal bird slammed into the left side of the home where the guards had quarters. This caused a secondary explosion that made the roof on that side of the home collapse while the entire structure filled with smoke and flames.

Soulless sped down the hill on his stolen police motorcycle and had the lights and siren going when he was back out on the county road. He needed to confirm his kill. When he reached the locked gate leading to Malone's compound, he removed a short-barreled shotgun from the backpack he wore and used it to destroy the lock.

Black smoke was billowing into the sky from the scene of the jet crash and devastated house. Of the fifteen people who had been in and around the home, only four had managed to survive. One of them was Franco Malone. No one from the plane crash had lived.

The survivors were gathered together a couple of hundred feet from the scene of disaster. Other than a hacking cough from inhaling smoke, Malone appeared well. One of his three remaining guards lay on the ground writhing in terrible pain from his injuries. He had severe burns to the right side of his body, but the other two guards had escaped the flames and were coughing like Malone. The men's pale faces revealed that they were shaken by the loss of their friends and colleagues. They had also suffered a close call with death.

Soulless was dressed as a cop and was riding a police motorcycle. The two guards who were still on their feet took him to be a first responder to the scene and not a threat. Soulless slowed the motorcycle and coasted up to them. Their looks of surprise were almost comical when Soulless brought up his gun and shot each of them twice in the chest. The remaining guard, the one with the burns, raised up a hand while moaning. Soulless dispatched him with a single shot to the head.

Franco Malone, unarmed, had taken off running. Soulless pursued him on the motorcycle and sent Malone sprawling by bumping him lightly with the bike's front wheel. Soulless was off the motorcycle before Malone made it to his feet.

The drug kingpin turned his head and looked up at Soulless while positioned on his hands and knees. He saw only the mirrored surface of the motorcycle helmet gazing back at him.

"Whatever you were paid to kill me, I can pay more."

Soulless answered Malone by shooting him in the side. After Malone rolled over onto his back, Soulless placed a round between his eyes. The contract was fulfilled.

Before leaving, Soulless extracted a gold coin, an American Eagle, from his pocket and placed the shiny money inside Malone's mouth. It marked the man as one of his kills. Had he been a lesser target, the coin would have been made from silver. It had been a while since Soulless had used the silver coins. His growing reputation had him being offered high-value targets of late.

A car driven by a sheriff's deputy was approaching the entrance to the driveway as Soulless was exiting it. Soulless ignored the new arrival and rocketed away from the scene.

The motorcycle was abandoned at the rear of a strip mall where Soulless had parked a car earlier. The lone security camera overhead had been disabled and there was no one else around.

Soulless tossed the motorcycle helmet, police jacket, and his gloves into a dumpster, then set fire to it all. Although the contract on Malone was done, there were still loose ends that had to be handled.

Tonya Vickers massaged her feet as she sat sideways in a booth at the restaurant she worked in. She had just finished a ten-hour shift of waitressing and couldn't wait to get home and relax with a book before going to sleep. It had been a busy night and she had made great tips but being on her feet for so long was more tiring than it used to be.

She had taken the waitress job as a way to earn money while she went to school. Eight years later, she had a useless liberal arts degree and was still waitressing. During those years, she had worked at an advertising agency for a period and discovered that it paid less than her waitress job. She also didn't like the work or the people she had to deal with. On the weekends, she made almost as much money in tips waitressing as she did writing ad copy. She returned to being a full-time waitress and never looked back. And yet, the work was wearying. She didn't think it was something she would want to do much longer and was considering becoming a real estate agent. One of her friends, a former waitress, had gotten her license the year before and had sold six houses in an affluent area. That had earned her more than Tonya made in two years. Tonya sighed. She'd give it more thought and maybe make a change next year. There was no hurry. She was still young.

A shout came from the restaurant's kitchen. It

was followed by the clatter of metal pans hitting a tiled floor. The restaurant was closed, and the only ones left were Tonya, a few of the kitchen staff, and the owner/manager, Gerardo.

Tonya put her shoes back on and went to see what all the commotion was about. As she pushed through a set of swinging doors, she saw a man standing near the deep fryers wearing a ski mask. Tonya's mouth opened in shock as she realized they were being robbed.

"There's not much money here, mister. Most people pay with credit cards."

"I know," the man said. As he spoke, he raised his arm. Tonya saw the gun in his hand but was shot dead before her brain could process the faint noise of the suppressed rounds that ended her life. Her body dropped to the floor. She was still young. Several yards away from Tonya lay the corpses of her coworkers. They were also young and had had plans that they'd delayed implementing. No one was promised tomorrow.

AFTER KILLING TONYA, SOULLESS FOUND THE manager, Gerardo, in his cubbyhole of an office. Gerardo was in his forties, chubby, and wore glasses. He had a set of headphones on. The music that leaked out of the tiny speakers sounded like disco. On Gerardo's desk was a ledger book and a laptop computer. Behind the desk was an open safe. Gerardo noticed Soulless and jerked in his seat as he took in his masked face. He removed the headphones.

"You're robbing me?" When he noticed the gun, Gerardo raised his hands. "I'll give you money. Just don't hurt anyone."

Soulless walked over to the desk and stood beside Gerardo. "I want the hard drive from your security cameras. I also want you to access and erase any files related to the cameras."

"Okay, okay, okay," Gerardo said. "I'll give you everything from the cameras, you take the money, and we're all good, right?"

"That's right," Soulless said. There was money in the safe. Four bundles of banded bills. Soulless reached in and took them as Gerardo used the laptop to retrieve the files where previous security footage was stored.

"We only keep two weeks' worth of video," Gerardo said. "I'll wipe it now."

"And the hard drive?" Soulless asked.

Gerardo pointed to a bookcase. "It's on the third shelf there."

Soulless unplugged the hard drive and tucked it under his left arm. He would destroy it later.

Gerardo finished wiping the archival files from the cloud. Soulless told him to hand over his wallet and cell phone. Gerardo did so without hesitation. He was certain that Soulless would be satisfied and was about to leave. After all, the man was wearing a mask. No one could identify him. Gerardo was right that Soulless was leaving, but wrong in his assumption that Soulless had no reason to harm him.

Gerardo, like the waitress, Tonya, had seen Soulless on more than one occasion while he had dined with Heather. Soulless couldn't take the chance that they might give his description to anyone investigating Heather's death.

Soulless shot Gerardo dead with a weapon that was different from the one he had used to kill Tonya. After gathering up the laptop, he returned to the kitchen to take the wallets and phones of the dead there. The police would assume that two separate shooters had robbed the restaurant while killing the staff. They should have no reason to connect the slayings to the carnage out at Malone's compound.

Soulless left the restaurant and drove back to his hotel room. On the way there, he would dispose of the wallets and cell phones of the people he had just killed, along with the hard drive and laptop from Gerardo's office.

The contract on Malone was fulfilled and anyone

who could identify him had been eliminated. Soulless smiled with satisfaction at a job well done. His work as an assassin was the most important thing in his life, and it was work he enjoyed. There was only one man who was considered to be his superior. A man named Tanner.

2

THE CONTRACT

WASHINGTON, D.C.

AFTER SPENDING TIME OBSERVING THE AREA HE WAS visiting, Tanner entered an office building on K Street. Three muscular men in suits studied him as he approached the reception desk. They had the look of former military and were armed with Glock 19s. Tanner guessed that they were secret service agents or some other type of government bodyguards.

The young blonde behind the reception desk looked Tanner over as well and smiled, having liked what she'd seen. The name plate on her desk identified her as Jessica.

She asked Tanner who he had come to see.

25

"I'm here to see Thomas Lawson."

"And you are?"

"Expected," Tanner said. He was in a less than pleasant mood. Although he was in Washington to see Lawson and hoped to be offered a challenging contract, a part of him wanted to be back on his ranch with his family. It hadn't helped that his flight into Washington had been plagued by bad weather and severe turbulence.

After Tanner's refusal to identify himself, the receptionist's smile faded to be replaced by a more professional demeanor. The woman made a call that was answered right away.

"The visitor you were expecting is here to see you, but he won't give his name," Jennifer said. After pausing to listen, she smiled up at Tanner again. "Oh yes. His eyes are very sexy." Another pause, and then she said goodbye and hung up the phone. "Someone will be down to greet you and escort you upstairs," she told Tanner.

"Thank you."

"Hey buddy. Why can't you just give Jessica your name?"

That question was asked by one of the three men in suits. Tanner turned to look at him but said nothing.

"It's all right, Vince," Jessica said. "I don't need to know his name."

Vince walked over and stood in front of Tanner, whom he towered over. He also carried thirty more pounds of muscle to go with the height.

"He was rude to you. I don't like people being rude to you. I want him to tell you his name."

One of the other men spoke up. "Vince, stand down. Remember what Tony said about your temper."

Vince waved that off and moved closer to Tanner. "Give the woman your name before I make you do it."

Tanner ignored him and remained silent. When Vince's hand shot out to give him a shove, Tanner leaned sideways to avoid it, then gripped the thumb on Vince's outstretched hand. He gave it a vicious twist as he took out the concealed weapon he carried. Vince had opened his mouth to cry out in pain and Tanner shoved the barrel of his gun into it. At the same time, he used his left hand to free Vince's gun, a Glock, from its holster. He rested his arm on Vince's shoulder and aimed the Glock at a spot between the other two men, then issued a warning.

"Point your weapons at me and I'll kill your friend before using his body as a shield."

The two agents had their hands on their weapons but had yet to draw them from their holsters.

Tanner's actions had been so swift and unexpected that they'd barely had time to react.

Vince jerked his head back in an attempt to free Tanner's gun from his mouth. It didn't work. Tanner had anticipated the move and kept the weapon firmly lodged, which caused Vince to gag. Still seated behind her reception desk, Jessica's eyes were wide with wonder and her face had turned pale.

A glance at the bank of elevators revealed that one of them was about to reach the level of the lobby. Tanner wondered if it would be filled with more armed agents. There were cameras in the lobby. Someone must be observing the scene.

The standoff continued and the elevator beeped just before the doors opened. Standing inside the car was the familiar face of a young woman. Despite her youth, she had a mane of brilliant white hair. Shock flitted across her features for a moment, to be replaced by a smile. Her name was Rhona O'Donnell. She was Thomas Lawson's apprentice.

"I see you've met the security staff. Please don't kill them."

"The one with the gun in his mouth tried to shove me. I don't think he'll try it again," Tanner said. He removed the weapon from Vince's mouth and sent him stumbling backwards with a kick to the gut. The big man's feet became tangled and he fell on his ass. He bounced up, red with rage, and breathing heavy. Tanner lowered his arms and let the weapons point toward the floor.

Rhona spoke to the agents. "I don't know what happened and I don't care, but this man is not to be harmed. Is that clear?"

Vince glared at Tanner and said nothing. His good hand was cradling the one with the injured thumb. His companions told Rhona they understood and relaxed, letting their hands slide off the butts of their weapons. The sound of running footsteps came from a nearby corridor and two men appeared holding rifles. Rhona called to the older of them.

"It's all right, Tony."

Tony, the agent-in-charge, stared at the guns in Tanner's hands, but neither he nor the other man made a threatening move with the rifles. In any other situation he would have demanded that the man in front of him drop his weapons. This was different. He was assigned to protect Thomas Lawson and Rhona O'Donnell. They gave the orders. If Miss O'Donnell had no problem with her guest being armed, then he had to accept that.

Looking past Tanner, Tony saw Vince's red face and frowned. He'd walked inside the security office after having gone across the hall for a cup of coffee. When he'd looked up at the monitors, he had seen Tanner knocking Vince to the floor.

"What happened here?"

The agent who had warned Vince to stand down explained what had transpired. He put the blame for the situation squarely on Vince.

"Go to the office, Vince," Tony said. "We need to talk."

"This wasn't my fault. That asshole was rude to Jessica."

Tony pointed at Tanner. "This man is a guest of Mr. Lawson and Miss O'Donnell. He is none of your concern. And you've been warned about your temper. Get to the office now; I'll be along soon."

Vince stalked off down the corridor Tony had come from. Before leaving, he gave Tanner a look that carried the promise of menace.

Tanner held out Vince's weapon to Tony, who accepted it as he spoke to Rhona. "I apologize for my man's behavior, Miss O'Donnell. It won't happen again."

Rhona answered with a nod and wrapped her arm through Tanner's, to lead him to the elevator. As the doors closed, Tanner asked her a question.

"Were you the one the receptionist spoke to on the phone?"

"Yes."

"Good. I was hoping that Thomas hadn't described my eyes as sexy."

Rhona laughed and asked him how he had been since they'd last seen each other the year before.

Tanner said he was fine and curious about what Thomas had to offer him.

"I take it that it's a difficult contract, yeah?"

Rhona let out a sigh before speaking. "Difficult and very dangerous, but I'll let Thomas give you the details. He was a bit surprised that you didn't ask for them before agreeing to come here."

"I owe Thomas. If he wants a favor, I'll do what I can to give it to him."

The elevator pinged and they stepped out to enter another reception area. There was no one behind the desk, but a pair of Marines stood guard at a set of oak double doors.

They greeted Rhona with a nod while eyeing Tanner. Rhona input a five-digit code into a keypad and led Tanner past the doors.

Thomas Lawson stood in front of an enormous monitor that hung on a wall. He turned and greeted Tanner with a smile.

"Thank you for coming, Tanner."

"I'll be there anytime you need me, Thomas."

Lawson's hair was a bit whiter than the last time Tanner had seen him, but he looked as if he had more vitality. Years earlier, Lawson was kidnapped and nearly killed. The ordeal had taken a toll on him. It had also left him with neurological damage. Lawson required the use of a cane to get around.

After shaking his hand and asking Tanner if he

wanted anything to drink or eat, the three of them settled down at a table that already had a carafe of coffee and three cups on it. Tanner poured a cup of the brew and sipped at it.

Lawson sent Rhona a nod and she tapped at a keyboard. A map of Africa appeared on the monitor with a red dot in the southern region.

"Are you familiar with the name Mohamed Kwami, Tanner?" Lawson asked.

The name did ring a bell. After a moment of thought, Tanner answered. "Would that be General Kwami, the dictator of Malika?"

"Exactly."

"He was the one who built an army of child soldiers back in the 1990s. Some of them were as young as five if I remember right."

"You do. He ended that practice and lost control of part of his country. That region renamed itself Dubabi and is independent of the general. Strangely enough, seventeen of those original child soldiers have grown up to become General Kwami's personal bodyguards. They are in their thirties, with one in his forties. As sick as it is, the general is a father figure to them. They help him maintain his iron grip on Malika and keep their people under his thumb."

"You want him dead? Is that why I'm here?"

"Yes."

"Why now?"

Rhona spoke up. "Malika is a tiny country but it's sitting atop a huge deposit of platinum. Platinum is a strategic metal that could give an advantage to the country that controls that mine. General Kwami would make deals with our enemies. If he were out of the picture, we would have an opportunity to gain control of that asset through allies on the African continent, possibly even his son."

"The general has a son?"

"He had him late in life. Juda Kwami is only twenty-four and known as the Prince of Malika. The general allows him to run certain aspects of the government. The prince went to school in England and is behind a cultural and technological resurgence in the country. His people and the world would be better off if he were in charge instead of his father."

Tanner held up a hand. "I don't care about the politics, Rhona. The general is worthy of a contract because of what he's done to his people, especially the children. I'll kill him for you. What happens afterwards doesn't concern me."

"Fair enough," Rhona said. "But know that killing General Kwami might be the most difficult assassination you've ever attempted. The man is not only guarded by his core seventeen bodyguards, but he also has dozens of men watching over him, mercenaries. He hasn't been seen in public in four years. Now that he's begun mining for the platinum, he has to know that he's a target. That means the men guarding him will be on alert."

"Why is he using mercenaries as guards and not the army?"

"Two reasons," Lawson said. "There was an attempted coup by a group of army personnel that the general put down several years ago. Since that time, he's been wary of them. Other than the ex-child soldiers, no one from his military is allowed to have direct physical contact with him."

"And what's the second reason for the mercs?"

Rhona answered. "The general used mercenaries supplied by a friend to protect the palace in the aftermath of the coup attempt. That practice continues. The man in charge of the mercenaries is Wes Walker; he's a white man from South Africa. The general trusts him."

"Do you accept the contract?" Lawson asked.

"Yes, Thomas."

"Thank you. We'll pay your usual fee and provide you with as much support and assistance as you need."

"I'll take all the intel you can give me, but it will be best if no one else knows that I'm traveling to Africa."

Rhona tapped at the keyboard again and a photo of General Mohamed Kwami appeared. "He may have aged some since this photo was taken five years ago. He'll be turning seventy-two in four months."

"No, he won't," Tanner said.

Lawson and Rhona shared a look as they took his meaning. Tanner had accepted the contract on the general. General Kwami didn't know it, but he was a dead man.

TANNER LEFT THE BRIEFING AND EXITED THE BUILDING over an hour later. He had to call Sara and tell her about the contract. Killing General Kwami would mean that he'd be away from home for quite some time. Rhona was right when she said that it would be a difficult assassination. Having to be separated from his family for so long only made it more arduous.

It was September. The weather on the late summer day was pleasant as the temperature was in the seventies and the humidity level was low. The hotel that had been arranged for him was only a few miles away. Tanner decided to walk there as he went over the information he had just been given.

He hadn't gone more than two blocks when he realized that a car, a dark-blue coupe, was creeping along in the right lane. The vehicle had its hazard lights on, and a hand was sticking out of the window, urging the drivers behind the car to go around. Was it someone looking for an address, perhaps a driver experiencing car trouble, or something else? Something to do with him.

Other than the arm sticking out the window, the driver was obscured behind tinted glass. It was a man's arm and he appeared to be wearing a suit jacket. Tanner entered a shop that sold vitamins. The place was busy. Like the car, the storefront had tinted windows.

He tried to get a look at the driver but was still unable to do so. The sporty vehicle had stopped moving and was double-parked. It appeared that it was waiting for him to emerge from the store. Tanner walked along the shelves. He kept watch on the car while pretending to browse. As he stood in front of a display of organic sea kelp, he made a call.

Rhona answered on the first ring. She must have recognized the number because the phone Tanner was using was one she had given to him during the briefing.

"I might have picked up a tail."

"You're being followed?"

"Yeah, and I have an idea who it is. Find out what kind of car that security guard, Vince, drives."

"Vince? Could he be that stupid?"

"That's the impression I got."

Rhona asked him to hold. She came on the line again moments later with the information.

"His full name is Vince Mercer. Tony says he drives a blue Dodge Challenger. He also told me that he placed Vince on suspension."

"It looks like I guessed right."

"Tell me where you are, and I'll have Tony handle it."

"I can handle it."

"Will Vince still be breathing afterwards?"

"That depends on him."

Rhona asked Tanner where he was, and he told her. She said she was sending someone to deal with it.

"Let Tony handle it. We don't need you involved in an incident that will attract the police."

"That won't work."

"Why not?"

"Vince is headed toward me now."

Vince was stepping out of his sports car with a scarf wrapped around his face. It hid everything but his eyes. As he approached the vitamin shop his hand slipped beneath his jacket, where a gun was holstered on his hip. Tanner saw the plan. Vince would enter the shop pretending to be a robber and shoot Tanner, making him look like an innocent victim of a robbery gone wrong. Tanner pretended not to have noticed him and moved swiftly down the aisle and through a pair of hanging curtains. He had entered a small space that had a desk on one side and shelving on the other. Straight ahead was a red door that led to the parking area behind the row of shops. The vitamin store was located on a corner. Tanner unlocked a rear door, ran out to the side street, and circled back to the front of the store.

VINCE HAD TAKEN OUT HIS GUN AND WAS brandishing it at the people nearest the entrance. They were raising their hands in the air, as the cashier emptied the cash drawer and tossed money onto the counter.

"Take it and go. There's no need to use that gun."

Vince wasn't listening. His eyes were darting about as he looked for Tanner. The door opened behind him and a bell chimed. When Vince spun around, he saw Tanner pointing a gun at him. Tanner fired three times and hit Vince in the chest. The maverick secret service agent collapsed to the floor, his gun slipping from his fingers.

Several of the women in the store had screamed. Tanner held up a set of credentials and told them that he was a federal agent. It was a lie, but he did have ID that identified him as a homeland security agent. He used it often when flying commercial, as it allowed him to skip a trip through the scanners. It was identification that Thomas Lawson had given him years earlier.

Tanner opened the door and told the customers to leave. The woman working the register and two other employees stepped outside with them, eager to get away from a scene of violence. They hurried past Vince's crumpled form as if he were radioactive.

Vince was lying on the floor moaning, but there was no blood. The bulletproof vest he wore had protected him and kept him alive.

A car screeched to a stop outside. It was driven by the agent named Tony. Rhona was with him. Sirens could be heard approaching; the police had been called.

Rhona entered the shop and looked down at Vince. "He's alive?"

"I shot him in the vest. I felt it earlier when we were in the lobby of the office building."

"What if he had taken it off?"

"Then he'd be dead instead of going to jail. I'm good with either outcome."

Tanner told Rhona and Tony about Vince's robbery ploy. After cuffing his hands behind his back, Tony stood over Vince with a look of disgust on his face.

"I knew you had a bad temper. I didn't know that you were a complete moron. Even your uncle won't get you out of this jam."

"Who is his uncle?" Tanner asked.

"He's a congressman, and the only reason Vince here was ever given a chance."

The police arrived and the situation was sorted out. Tony went outside with the cops as two officers hustled Vince into the back of an ambulance. Vince was getting medical attention because of the pain Tanner's rounds were causing him. Rhona stayed behind with Tanner inside the shop. She smiled up at him.

"Does trouble follow you everywhere you go?"

"Like a shadow," Tanner said.

3
THE COMPETITION

THE UNITED STATES WASN'T THE ONLY GOVERNMENT interested in gaining control of General Kwami's platinum mine. Like the U.S., a foreign power in the Arabian Peninsula knew that the general had to be dealt with before anyone could make a move that would give them command of the valuable asset.

Having made a name for himself as a top assassin, Soulless was contacted and offered the contract on the general. He accepted without hesitation. Killing General Kwami would be the biggest challenge of his career. The fee he received was commensurate with the risk and was more than he had ever earned for killing.

Soulless was living in Chicago when the contract came in. He traveled often and never had his own apartment. Hotels and motels were where he laid his head, but never the same one two nights in a row unless he couldn't avoid it. Occasionally, he would live with a woman. He didn't make a practice of that too often however; once he decided to move on, he would invariably kill the woman he'd been sleeping with so that she couldn't identify him. When that became necessary, he dispatched them painlessly while they were sleeping, then set fire to their apartments or homes to expunge any trace of his DNA.

Often, there was no reason to think that his lover would ever be asked about him. Still, Soulless gave extra care to maintaining his anonymity. He had been burned in the past and would not like to repeat the experience.

His employer had offered to coordinate his travel arrangements to Africa and also supply him with a false ID and passport. Soulless declined and let them know that he would handle such things himself.

He had made valuable contacts on the black-market and could order what he needed over the internet. As for arming himself once he was on the ground in Africa, that shouldn't prove too difficult. After all, there were guns everywhere.

What Soulless needed most was a plan, a way to kill his target. Soulless had been supplied with all the information his employer had gathered on General Kwami and his security. He had even been given detailed plans of Kwami's palace and a series of reports concerning facts that might help him. The small country of Malika had been in the control of the British government before World War I. As a result, English was spoken there along with the country's native tongue. France had extensive business interests in Malika before the general rose to power and had employed most of the country. Consequently, many older residents also spoke French. Soulless could speak either language fluently, along with his native language of Russian. Communication should not be a problem.

Soulless ordered food from room service along with a pot of coffee. When it came, he answered the door while wearing a robe and pretending to dry his hair with a towel. The young man who delivered the food never got a good look at his face and received an average tip that wouldn't make Soulless memorable.

After eating, Soulless drank coffee as he went over the material he'd been given. By the time it grew dark outside, he had the beginnings of a plan that would end with him placing a gold coin between the dead lips of General Kwami.

TANNER WAS INSIDE HIS OWN HOTEL ROOM IN Washington. He was seated on the side of his bed while talking to Sara over a secure line. She had known that he would accept Lawson's offer of a contract; she wasn't prepared for what Tanner told her about it.

"You'll be gone for weeks?"

"I think so. The target is heavily guarded, and I'll have to come up with a way to get to him. There's still the problem of having a reason for being in the country. Malika is over ninety-five percent black. I'll stand out there and I don't speak the native language. There's also little transportation other than cars and there are few roads. The general controls the military, the police, and everything else. His death will cause an uproar and make whoever kills him a sought-after prize. There's an open bounty on anyone who so much as insults the general. When I kill him that reward will be for more money than most people there make in a lifetime."

"Getting away may be more difficult than fulfilling the contract."

"I'll have help there thanks to Thomas. Once the general is dead I'll be airlifted out of the country."

"It all sounds very dangerous, Cody."

"It is, but that's what makes it exceptional. I've

trained most of my life to be able to do things like this. I look forward to the challenge."

Sara was quiet for a moment, then she asked a question. "Do you have a plan?"

"I've come up with two possibilities. They would both take time to get going. The general is aware that he's a target and doesn't even trust his own military. He'll be wary of strangers and will have someone watching out for newcomers to the country who travel near the palace. Although the general's son has made the country more modern, Malika isn't exactly a tourist destination. People don't visit there for no reason."

"I'll miss you, and so will Lucas and Marian."

"How are they?"

"They're good, but both are asleep."

"I'll try to call home as often as I can, but there might be several days at a time when I won't be able to call."

"I understand. Don't worry about us. Concentrate on what you need to do. When are you leaving for Africa?"

"That depends on what plan I choose to work on. Right now, I'm leaning toward one that will see me making a detour to England."

"Why England?"

"The general's personal guards are some of his former child soldiers. The other men guarding him arc supplied by the man he buys his weapons from. They go back many years. That man is based in London, where he recruits mercenaries."

"And you want to be one of those mercenaries?"

"Yeah. That way, there's a chance that I'll be shipped off to Malika. Lawson learned that the general is beefing up his defenses."

"Is the general this arms dealer's only client?"

"No. But if I'm assigned to another client, I'll switch to Plan B."

"And what's that?"

"I'll try to get hired at the platinum mine. It's only miles away from the general's palace and will give me an excuse to be in the country."

"Posing as a mercenary suits you better."

"I think so too."

Tanner talked to Sara for a little longer prior to saying goodnight. Before hanging up, he told her he loved her and to kiss their children for him. He'd been separated from his son and daughter for less than a day and missed them already. Little Marian had just turned eight months old and Lucas was Cody's shadow when he was home on the ranch. Being away from his family for so long a period would be a sacrifice.

Tanner closed his eyes and cleared his mind of such thoughts. He had a contract to fulfill and needed to keep his focus on his work. He lay in bed and used a laptop to study the native tongue of the Malikan people. He couldn't become fluent in it in a matter of days, but thanks to his natural gift for learning languages, he could teach himself a few key phrases so that he wouldn't be completely ignorant of what might be said around him. The more he knew, the better off he would be.

After two hours of study he went to sleep. He had to catch a flight to London the next day.

In Chicago, Soulless had come to the same conclusions that Tanner had reached. He agreed that becoming a bodyguard or working in the mine were the two best ways to get near the general. Unlike Tanner, working in the mine had been Soulless's first choice. That is, it would become such if he was able to acquire needed information. He had asked his client to assist him with that.

He had just stepped out of the shower when a call came in and he was given a name, a time, and a place to meet someone who could help him. The place was Cape Town, South Africa, and the time was two days hence. As for the man he was meeting, he was a former miner who had worked in Malika decades earlier when the French still had business interests in the country. One of those businesses had been in control of a pair of copper mines.

The largest of those mines was where the general had built his palace, while the smaller mine was where platinum had been found. The former miner would have valuable information that Soulless could use.

Soulless had a plan to kill General Kwami. Like most of his plans, it involved the death of many. If Soulless were a fisherman, he'd be the type to use dynamite rather than a colorful lure.

He rested his head on the pillow and drifted off to sleep. Like Tanner, he had no doubt that he would kill the general. One of them would be disappointed.

4

PREPARATIONS AND PLANS

WHILE ON THE FLIGHT TO LONDON, TANNER USED the time to go over the material Lawson had given him concerning General Kwami's palace. The word palace usually conjures up images of a grand structure climbing high into the sky with gold and gleaming spires. The general's "palace" was a far cry from that.

While it was a huge structure that contained over fifty rooms it was only one story tall, made of red brick, and was spread out across acres of land. It had been built inside the massive pit that had once been a copper mine.

The pit was oval in shape and over a mile in diameter. Kwami's palace was at the bottom of it with the pit's high sides making a stone barrier. Above that barrier a wall had been erected along with a massive iron gate. An aerial photo showed that armed guards patrolled the rim of the pit with more guards protecting the single road that led to the palace.

While at first glance erecting the palace inside the open pit appeared to be a clever way to enhance security, Tanner had remarked that it also made it hard for anyone inside to escape if needed. Once the road was controlled by an enemy, anyone inside the palace would be trapped.

That was when Tanner learned from Thomas Lawson that there was a rumor General Kwami had an escape tunnel in the palace. Mining had been going on in the area since the English controlled the region over a century ago.

Miles away where the platinum mine was located was a second pit that was smaller than the one the palace occupied. Mining had left a maze of tunnels between the two pits. It was believed that one or more extended between the pits and connected them.

"There are numerous caverns, tunnels, and old ore tracks running beneath the pit from earlier ore mining; perhaps as many as a hundred different passageways," Lawson had said. "It seems likely that the general and his core of ex-soldiers have created a way to access one of them. If you allow him the time to do so, he might slip away from the palace."

Tanner had nodded his agreement. When he came at the general, he would have to do so without raising an alarm. At the very least, he couldn't cause such a threat that the man would panic and seek escape. Given that he had so many men protecting him, it seemed likely that fleeing the palace through an underground tunnel would be a last resort for General Kwami.

TANNER CHECKED INTO A HOTEL ROOM IN LONDON under the name of Brett Foxx. The hour was late, but the bars were still open. He decided to hit the ground running.

The arms dealer that supplied General Kwami with weapons was named Ayo Kenyatta. Kenyatta and the general had been boyhood friends in the slums of Malika. They had both made successes of themselves and left the gutter behind. Neither man had ever given a thought to how their actions affected others.

Kenyatta did business at a bar he owned in the Southwark district. The intel stated that the bar was a marketplace of sorts where one could buy a gun or hire someone to burn down a building. If you were in good with the owner, Kenyatta, you could even purchase a crate of rifles.

Kenyatta was also a recruiter of armed bodyguards. The men he hired weren't interested in standing sentry inside a jewelry store all day. They were men who looked forward to being tested and would protect their clients with the use of lethal force.

Under his identity of Brett Foxx, Tanner was being vouched for by a business associate of Kenyatta's. The associate was a money launderer who had branched out into the drug world and found himself in trouble with the UK's National Crime Agency. In order to make those charges go away, the money launderer was cooperating with authorities. Lawson had arranged for Tanner's endorsement to be a part of that cooperation.

Kenyatta had very dark skin, was small and bony, and had a head of white hair. As Tanner approached the booth he was seated in, two large men stepped in front of him.

One of the men looked Tanner over as he spoke to him. "This area is private."

Tanner smiled and nodded toward Kenyatta. "I just came over to introduce myself. Mr. Kenyatta and I have a mutual acquaintance." Tanner mentioned the name of the money washer and saw the older man acknowledge him with a nod.

Kenyatta spoke. "He said to expect someone. You are American?"

"That's right."

"And you want to be a bodyguard?"

"Yes sir. Somewhere out of the UK if possible." Tanner smiled. "I've worn out my welcome here, so to speak."

Kenyatta reached out a wrinkled hand and tapped the man standing closest to him. "Get his phone number and add him to the list."

"I'm in?" Tanner asked.

Kenyatta smiled, revealing crooked and stained teeth. "You can try out. I only choose the best."

"Fair enough. When are the tryouts?"

"Soon. You'll get a call sometime in a day or two telling you where to go."

"Thanks," Tanner said. He then gave Kenyatta's man a number where he could be reached. After sending the old man a nod, Tanner headed back to the bar where he sipped on a beer and feigned interest in the soccer game that was playing on the TV.

He left the bar an hour later to return to his hotel room and call home. It was six hours earlier back at the ranch and he wanted to talk to his children before they were put to bed by Sara. After making the call he realized he was feeling homesick. It was not an emotion he liked.

53

THE NEXT DAY, SOULLESS KEPT HIS MEETING WITH THE old man who had once been a miner in Malika. He was after information that would help him kill the general. They sat together at a table inside the Central Library of Cape Town and spoke quietly.

The old man was Mr. Tersoo. He had to be nearing eighty, but his dark skin was fitted onto a frame that was still muscular from a lifetime of hard labor. His brown eyes were alert and indicated that his memory would be good. Soulless passed over an envelope that contained an agreed upon sum. It was a pittance to Soulless but a small fortune to the old man.

Soulless was wearing a fake beard, a wig, and sunglasses to hide his features. If he had met with Mr. Teesoo undisguised, he would have felt the necessity to kill the man afterwards.

Teesoo spoke English with an accent but was easily understandable. He was also well-spoken for someone who'd likely had little education. The fact that the old man had asked to meet inside a library might explain that.

Soulless asked him about the mine shafts and tunnels that ran beneath the palace in Malika. He was wondering how difficult it might be to use one of them to find a way to tunnel up and into the general's lair.

Mr. Teesoo smiled as he shook his head. "There is

a honeycomb of tunnels in that area, many of which go nowhere. The mining company hired incompetents who were related to the owner and put them in charge. I remember they had us digging in a very haphazard manner."

"Why?"

"We stumbled upon a small vein of gold. After that, we were allowed overtime to search for other deposits. I would guess that we dug scores of shafts while looking for more gold. We found none. Some of those dead-end tunnels go on for hundreds of meters."

Like Tanner, Soulless was aware that General Kwami had an escape route that relied on using one of the old mine shafts. If what Mr. Teesoo said was true, finding that one tunnel might be nearly impossible. Soulless was disappointed by what he was learning, but not deterred. It just meant that he would have to adjust his tactics.

"You say that it's like a honeycomb beneath that old copper mine where the palace was built. Do you mean that literally?" Soulless asked.

The old man nodded. "Much digging went on there after the copper mine was abandoned. There were two copper mines, but the smaller one is now being used to search for platinum."

"Those pits are deep. Why didn't they find the platinum before now?"

"Those depressions, the pits, where the palace was built, and the smaller mining pit are a result of the way the copper was mined. It's what is called an open pit. After that, long wall mining was done beneath the surface; what you know as tunneling. Breakthroughs in drilling have allowed miners to go deeper than when I was a miner. That's where those deposits of platinum are."

"How dangerous is it to enter those mines?"

"It was all very dangerous work in my day, and we lost men in cave-ins. I survived a cave-in once. That was when I quit and found a different profession."

"What caused the cave-ins?"

"We were blamed by the company. They said we ignored the safety regulations." The old man laughed. "There were no regulations. We were handed a hard hat and a pick and told to dig. The real problem was the open pit mining that had already taken place above the tunnels. Such mining weakens the soil and damages the bedrock. But the men who ran the mine had dreams of gold. They didn't care what happened to us until it made their insurance costs go up."

Soulless questioned Mr. Teesoo for a few minutes more before thanking him and leaving the library. Once outside he gazed north where the country of Malika lay many miles away. It was a small nation, and one of over fifty that made up the African continent. And General Kwami was just another dictator in a list that numbered in the dozens worldwide. He was most notable for his brutality of having used children for soldiers and the fact that he had stayed in power for so long. Kwami's death would be noteworthy as well. Soulless would see to that.

It looked as if it would be unlikely that he'd be able to use the general's hidden tunnel to get to him. That was disappointing, but something Mr. Teesoo said had given Soulless another idea about how to approach the problem of killing the general. New plan or old, he would still need to access the mines. That meant he would have to get a job as a miner.

The mining company's headquarters was located in the Malikan city of Youshu. It had a population of twenty-two thousand and had become more welcoming of whites since the general's western-educated son brought his influence to bear.

The mining company gathered up unskilled laborers every Monday morning at the harbor, loaded them into a large flatbed truck, and drove them to the mine. Once there, they would live at the work camp for the week and be returned to the port on Friday night. Soulless was determined to become one of those laborers. It was necessary if the new plan he was formulating was to work. He would also need to contact his employer and request assistance. Items needed for his plan to succeed were far easier for them to come up with than if he had to acquire such things himself.

Soulless hailed a taxi and told the driver to take him to the harbor in Yousho. He wanted to explore the area before he showed up there in the morning to seek employment with the mining company. If he had to flee the port for any reason or find a place of concealment, he wanted to already know what to do.

Soulless didn't have friends, hobbies, or any family that he stayed in contact with. His work was the reason why he rose from bed each day. He wanted to someday be acknowledged as the greatest assassin of all time. The killing of General Kwami would go a long way toward him being able to lay claim to that title.

His thoughts turned to Tanner. The man had been inactive for months and Soulless wondered if perhaps he had retired. He hoped so. Tanner had his day. Now, it was his turn. He would take tougher and tougher contracts and kill each target until he became recognized as the best assassin who ever lived. In time, Tanner would be no more than a memory, like Maurice Scallato and Lars Gruber. Those men were also once thought to be the best.

Soulless would eclipse them all. It was the only

thing he wanted and nothing and no one would stop him.

After crossing the border checkpoint, the taxi dropped Soulless off at the port and he proceeded to walk the area. The phony beard itched a bit and he was thankful that it was a cool day. As he walked along, he thought more about the new plan he had come up with to kill General Kwami. It all relied on him getting hired on at the mine. The fact that he had no experience in the field never entered into his equation.

In the United States going to work in a mine required training, knowledge of safety procedures, and enrollment in an apprenticeship program. The standards in Malika were much laxer. If you had a pulse and were willing to work like a mule, you qualified. Soulless was fit, strong, and unafraid of hard work. Knowing that the job could be dangerous held no dread for him. The only thing Soulless feared was failure. It was something he hated with a passion. If anyone attempted to prevent him from fulfilling his contract, that person would die, be they a guard, the law, or the devil himself. Failure was not an option.

5
YOU, YOU, NOT YOU

Tanner received the call telling him when and where to arrive for his try out as an elite bodyguard. The when was seven a.m. The where was a secluded warehouse a few miles outside of London that had a fenced in field behind it.

The inside of the warehouse had been converted into a firing range. Outside in the field was an obstacle course and a running track. Five men handled the tryouts and acted as instructors. Tanner was one of twenty-eight hopefuls. That number was whittled down by a few after their lack of experience surfaced. Tanner's false identity had been supplied with a background that had him having seen action in South America, the Middle East, and Northern Africa.

More men were eliminated during the first test,

which was designed to see how fit they were. The test was similar to the one given to U.S. Marines. It involved a three-mile run, "dead hang" pull-ups, and abdominal crunches. Tanner was in peak condition and aced the test easily along with most of the other men, one of whom was a man named Colin Palmer. Palmer was English, and black. He was about Tanner's size and had a similar build but was a decade younger. The two of them had run the three miles in under fifteen minutes while finishing neck and neck. Palmer had sent Tanner a nod of acknowledgement after that and Tanner had answered it.

Some of the men who were bulkier with muscle failed the pull-up portion of the test with dismal attempts that saw them barely able to complete more than three repetitions. One man was unable to finish running the three miles.

Of the twenty-eight that started, seventeen moved on to the next test, which involved unarmed combat skills. This meant getting in a nine-foot-wide circle with another man. If you stepped out of the circle you lost. There was a time limit of two minutes. If both men stayed in the circle until the time ran out, both men moved on to the next test. Those not fighting stood by shoulder to shoulder in a line to watch the action.

Tanner faced off against a brute of a man, a

bearded German named Trager. When the instructor gave the word to begin, Trager charged at Tanner with his muscular arms extended, intending to shove him out of the circle. Tanner gripped the man's wrists, fell backwards, and used his feet to propel the German over him and into the air. Trager landed on his back in the grass with a thud that knocked the wind out of him. The bout took all of three seconds. When Tanner looked over at Palmer, he saw that he was smiling.

Palmer's opponent let it be known that he was a black belt in karate. If true, it did him little good. An instant after the signal was given to begin, Palmer landed a scissor kick on his opponent's chin that sent the man stumbling backwards and out of the circle.

Tanner was impressed by Palmer's speed as the kick was no more than a blur of motion. He whispered, "Well done," as Palmer walked by him to get back in line. Palmer answered with a "Thanks."

The man who'd been beaten rose to his feet and protested that he hadn't been ready. The main instructor told him he could go home.

"There's no such thing as being ready," the lead instructor told him, "only being prepared. When the shit gets real excuses mean nothing."

The black belt gave the instructor the finger and sulked as he walked away. Two more men displayed little skill at fighting hand-to-hand and were asked to leave. That left thirteen men, and everyone headed inside to the shooting range.

Each man was given a Glock 22 and two full magazines. Palmer proved to also be a marksman. The other men were above average as well. The final test involved field stripping your weapon and putting it back together. Tanner took note that Palmer beat him at the task by a full second while the others were still attempting to reassemble their guns. One of the men, a kid of about twenty, dropped the spring and made matters worse when he accidently kicked it while turning to pick it up. The spring rolled under a table. When the kid rose from the floor after reaching under the table to retrieve the spring, the instructor let him know that he could go.

The young man's shoulders slumped, and he nodded. The instructor told him that he'd give him a call the next time they needed someone. Dropping the spring had been careless, but having it roll under the cart was just bad luck.

That left twelve men. The lead instructor told them that there were three clients who needed help. When he mentioned that one of the assignments was in the southern region of Africa, Tanner knew he was talking about General Kwami's compound.

"We're looking for six or more men to go there.

While there, you'll be on duty and expected to work long shifts. and you'll only get one day off every two weeks."

"What's it pay?" asked a thick man named Younger. He looked to be overweight but had run well and passed all the other tests.

The instructor explained that the compensation varied depending on your assignment. However, the base pay was higher than normal.

"That's good money," Younger said. "Sign me up."

"It gets better," the instructor told him. "If the client is attacked and you keep him breathing, you'll get a bonus so big you won't have to work for years."

"I'm interested," Tanner said, "but what are the other assignments?" Tanner didn't want to appear eager to sign up to guard the general. Also, it would only make sense that he'd want to know his other choices.

"One of the other assignments is here in the UK; the other will have you guarding a ship from pirates off the coast of Bangladesh."

Tanner looked as if he were thinking things over, then said that he was agreeable to go to Africa. Palmer raised up a hand, signaling that he was willing to accept that assignment as well.

When everything was settled, seven of them were being sent off to Africa. Younger snickered when he was told that he'd be guarding the general.

"I'm not surprised that someone wants him dead. I see why this gig pays well."

The lead instructor ignored him and continued giving out information.

"Be ready to travel at five a.m. two days from now. There will be a van sent to pick you up and take you to a private airfield. Pack light. Uniforms will be supplied to you once you're there. Good luck, mates."

As he was climbing into his rental to return to London, Tanner noticed that Palmer was looking at him as he stood beside a late-model Mercedes. After starting his engine, Tanner coasted his car over to speak to Palmer, who knew him as Brett Foxx.

"I guess we'll be working together."

"Looks that way," Palmer said.

"I'm glad. If there is trouble, I won't have to worry about you being able to handle it."

Palmer smiled. "I could say the same about you, Foxx."

Tanner sent him a nod and drove off slowly. Phase one of his plan to kill Kwami was done and he would soon be in Africa. That's when the hard part would begin.

SOULLESS'S PLANS HADN'T GONE AS SMOOTHLY AS Tanner's. When he showed up at the port, he found that he was one of over forty men looking to be hired on as a mine laborer. There were only five slots available. New slots opened up frequently, as the working conditions and heavy labor tended to cause men to quit and look for easier work.

Being white and a foreigner, he was one of the few non-blacks there. The man doing the hiring barely gave him a glance before picking others to fill his quota.

Moans of disappointment came from those not picked. Soulless wasn't disappointed. He was thinking. He'd understood that the odds of him being chosen were low and that he had to find a way to change that.

The men who were picked piled into the rear of a flatbed truck. Wooden benches had been bolted to the floor of the truck and dozens of men were pressed together on them. A metal frame had been attached to the truck bed and covered with a green tarp-like material. It helped to keep the wind off the men riding in the rear but did nothing against the chill.

The new miners were forced to settle on the floor in the midst of those seated. The man who did the choosing smiled at the ones he had failed to pick.

"Come back next week. We may need new men."

After saying that, he climbed into the front of the truck with the driver.

Soulless would return in a week. In the meantime, he would scheme to place the odds in his favor.

LIKE EVERY CITY IN THE WORLD, THE POLICE IN Malika had their favorite spots to eat when it was time to have lunch. At one restaurant, the cops parked in the rear and entered through the kitchen. The restaurant was owned by a retired policeman. He kept a private dining area off the kitchen so that his former colleagues could eat away from the crowd at the front of the restaurant. It was also a convenient way to pick up an order of food to take back to the station.

That task was handed off to less experienced officers. One of them was a young policeman named Kaden. Kaden left the rear of the restaurant holding a box that contained food for himself and other officers on duty.

He was standing at his car and set the box on the roof so he could open the door to get in. After reaching into his pocket to press a button on a key fob to unlock the door, he grabbed the box again.

Hands reached out from beneath the patrol

vehicle and gripped Kaden's ankles. He was yanked off-balance and sent falling backwards. Kaden released a yelp as hot coffee spilled from the box and burnt his right cheek. The stinging sensation had caused him to clench his eyes shut for a moment. When he opened them, he saw a man scrambling out from beneath his car. He registered the knife in the man's hand and panic bloomed. Kaden reached for his gun only to be stunned by an elbow to the face that left him with blurred vision. His attacker claimed his weapon and stood over him.

"Get up," the man said. He was a white man wearing a hooded sweatshirt. His face was unremarkable, and he was a little older than Kaden.

"You will be locked up for this," Kaden said. He was trying not to sound frightened, although he feared for his life.

"All I want are your weapons. Lean inside the car and free that shotgun from its rack."

The rifle in question was an R5 carbine. Kaden hesitated and the man took aim at his left leg.

"Get that rifle or I'll shoot you."

Kaden actually took comfort in the fact that the man had aimed at his leg. It indicated that he didn't want to kill him. He also realized the man spoke English with an American accent. That should make it easier to track him down afterwards.

"I have to reach into my pocket; I'll need my keys."

"Do it slowly."

Kaden took out the keys and leaned into the car to free the rifle. As he did so, the barrel of the gun was pressed against his side.

"Nice and easy. Don't make me shoot you."

Kaden handed the rifle back while still leaning into the car. The gun at his side was removed as the man yanked the rifle from his hand. An instant later, Kaden felt a stinging sensation across his throat and gasped in shock. Blood gushed from the fatal knife wound he'd received. Kaden's last rational thought before blind panic overtook him was that he would soon be dead.

SOULLESS PRESSED THE CAR DOOR AGAINST THE BACK of the cop whose throat he'd cut as the man thrashed about half-in and half-out of the patrol vehicle. The massive blood loss soon took its toll and the officer fell forward onto the front seats, which were now coated in red.

Soulless had what he needed—a rifle. He would use it to ensure that he would find a place on the next truck headed toward the mine.

~

FRIDAY EVENING FOUND SOULLESS RIDING A motorcycle as he trailed the flatbed truck ferrying the miners back to the city for the weekend. His murder of the cop had made the news, but they had failed to disclose that he'd taken more than a life. He had stolen a rifle.

Other than the time he'd spent on acquiring a weapon, the previous week had passed slowly. It was a wasted week and Soulless would be damned if he was going to waste another one and simply hope to be picked to work in the mine. He was going to stack the deck in his favor.

He sped up and passed the flatbed truck which was lumbering along in the slow lane. He could glimpse the faces of the last two men seated in the rear through the flap in the canvas covering they sat beneath. They appeared relaxed. They had pay in their pockets and were looking forward to their weekend away from the mine.

Soulless traveled twelve more miles before slowing the bike and taking an exit ramp. When he was off the highway, he tucked the motorcycle away in a fenced in area that held a small building. Inside the building was electrical equipment that controlled the streetlamps along the highway. Behind that was a hill that offered a view of the road.

There was thick brush there. Soulless had found the area earlier in the week and set up a shooting blind. He'd also traveled out to a remote area where he could become familiar with the R5 rifle. He was betting that he was good enough to hit a swiftly moving target.

He had rigged up a scope onto the police rifle. He used it to locate the truck in the oncoming traffic. As the truck grew closer, Soulless took in a breath, then released it slowly. Through the scope, he saw the man in the passenger seat, the same man who had failed to choose him to work in the mine. He was a stout man and his girth blocked Soulless's view of the thin man driving the truck. That was okay. A properly placed round should eliminate the problem.

Soulless pulled the trigger as the truck was almost even with his position. He had targeted a spot slightly ahead of where the truck was. His aim was perfect. The round entered through the side window, ripped through the right cheek of the man in the passenger seat, and kept going. The slug destroyed several teeth on the left side of the passenger's mouth as it exited, and then entered the rear of the driver's skull.

The vehicle crossed into another lane where it was struck by a pickup truck. After that it slammed into a light pole and flipped over to skid along the roadway. The men riding in the back were flung out of their seats and scattered along the road. The thin metal frame and the green tarp covering it had been no match for the weight of the men's bodies being slammed against it.

Several of the men died on impact from massive head injuries as they hit the roadway. The pickup truck's momentum caused it to keep traveling and it ran over two of the miners before coming to a stop. More vehicles became involved, and more of the miners were mangled beneath churning wheels.

One car slammed into the cab of the truck. The driver of the truck was dead, but the man who'd been shot in the mouth had still been alive. His body was crushed by the impact of the car, and the driver's body was also smashed.

The round fired by Soulless had exited out of the driver's head and would not be discovered. The massive accident would be blamed on the driver of the truck, although the reason for his carelessness would never be known. Blood tests would reveal that he was sober and not taking any drugs. Some would wonder if he'd fallen asleep, but due to the damage his body suffered in the wreck all trace of the rifle wound was obliterated. A fatal wound would not be suspected, and the true cause of the terrible event would remain a mystery.

SOULLESS ARRIVED AT THE PORT ON MONDAY morning. There was a new man hiring mine laborers. Instead of a paltry five positions to fill, he had twenty-six, since many of the former laborers had died or been severely injured in the traffic "accident."

The new driver was behind the wheel of a bus that had real seats and not a wooden bench. Soulless was chosen, took his seat on the bus, and was one step closer to killing the general.

6

SHOOTOUT

TANNER'S PLAN TO GET CLOSE TO THE GENERAL wasn't going as he'd hoped. While he was at the compound, he and Palmer had been given the job of patrolling the outer region surrounding the old mine basin where the palace had been erected.

Thanks to its location at the bottom of the huge pit, Tanner wasn't even in sight of the palace but was riding around in a Jeep keeping watch over a mostly flat and featureless landscape. To say the duty was tedious would be an understatement.

They had been given uniforms of a sort. A pair of tan khakis with matching shirts and caps. Tanner wore his usual black boots with the outfit. Each guard was given a Glock but only the guards walking the perimeter nearest the palace had rifles.

The one time he was near the palace was when

he was off-duty and at the barracks. It didn't help him any, as there were others around at all times and he was always in view of a camera. Sneaking out at night was an option, but there would still be the cameras, along with the risk that one of the other guards might see him leave.

All of that was known and could be handled. The difficulty came from that which he didn't know. He had no idea where the general's private quarters were inside the massive palace. He'd heard talk that it was located somewhere in the center but had yet to confirm that. Getting inside the palace would be a challenge and would require him to bypass numerous locks, alarms, cameras, guards, and soldiers. If an alarm sounded at any point while he was making his play to kill the dictator, the general could slip away by using the underground tunnel he reportedly had.

Getting to the general would not be done by force or daring. No, it would take guile and cleverness. Fortunately, they were qualities that Tanner possessed. When he had a plan in place, he would execute it. In the meantime, he did his job and kept his eyes and ears open.

The one bright spot was that he'd been paired with Palmer on his patrol. Like himself, Palmer spoke only when he had something to say. As a consequence, hours would pass in silence between them. Palmer wore a wedding band but never mentioned his wife. In his identity of Brett Foxx, Tanner was thought to be unmarried.

The closest they'd come to seeing action was when they spotted a dust cloud approaching. It turned out to be a trio of kids on dirt bikes. Seeing the boys made Tanner think of Henry.

A set of train tracks were along the southern section of their route. They were used by the processing plant that was affiliated with the platinum mine to the east. The excess rock from the mining operation was ground to a fine texture and turned into sand. After being loaded into the train cars, it was shipped south, eventually winding up in South Africa, where it would be sold.

So boring was the duty that Tanner found himself looking forward to the train's appearance. It seemed to be on a schedule that varied no more than fifteen minutes.

Before leaving Washington, D.C., Tanner had designated the train tracks as the place where he would be met by an extraction team once Kwami was dead. A helicopter was on standby to whisk him away after the hit was done. They could be summoned on an advanced two-way radio that had a range of forty miles. The radio and other supplies had been hidden near the train tracks in a prearranged spot by a covert team of operatives.

Without such help, escaping the country after the assassination would have been immensely more difficult. There were advantages to having the government as an ally.

Tanner hadn't spoken to Sara in nearly a week and had another week before he'd be able to do so. If there was a serious problem at home, Lawson had promised that he would make contact and General Kwami would be given a short reprieve until Tanner could return to deal with him. Tanner didn't expect that to happen. Sara was more than capable of handling herself. Also, she could call on Henry and Steve Mendez if threatened.

Being so far away from home and out of communication for such long stretches of time made Tanner aware that he needed to get going on one of the plans he had. He wanted to start a business that trained armed security guards. That way, there would always be men nearby who could respond if the ranch came under attack. The project had been put on hold as he had concentrated on his duties at the ranch.

He missed talking to Sara and his children. As a guard, he only got one day off every two weeks and cell and satellite phones weren't allowed. If he were caught with one, the best he could hope for would be to find himself fired. If the general suspected he had used the phone to communicate knowledge about the compound's defenses to an enemy, he'd simply be shot dead.

He had to find a way to get closer to Kwami while also being able to escape afterward. It would not be easy. Lawson's estimate about the strength of the general's security had been low. Tanner was one of eighty-two men guarding Kwami, and not the fifty-six that had been estimated. The number of guards varied slightly from day-to-day, depending on how many men were enjoying their day off.

On top of the regular guards, there were the seventeen former child soldiers who were at the general's side at all times. Each man was well-armed, and those who guarded the palace were given bulletproof vests to wear. As of yet, Tanner had no plan on how to kill his target. He needed more information. In order to get it, he had to maneuver himself into a position where he would be asked to guard the palace. For that, he would also need a plan, one that he wouldn't be able to implement without an element of luck and timing.

Tanner Five, Farnsworth, had often stated that providence would give you opportunities, but that most failed to take advantage of them because they lacked imagination. Tanner had found that to be true more often than not. What was certainly true is that he could use a bit of luck if he was going to kill General Kwami.

As usual, he had his head on a swivel and was aware of his surroundings as he drove along his route. They were near the northern border of Malika, beyond which lay the country of Dubabi, which had once been a part of Malika.

Dubabi's government had been overthrown three times in the last two years as political and religious factions battled for control. It was currently in a state of chaos with a group of rebels in power. An exodus of its well-off citizens was under way as crime and rocketing unemployment made the country unbearable for many people. They wisely migrated to regions other than Malika. The general had given orders that illegal immigrants be shot on sight.

Tanner spotted the approaching vehicles coming from Dubabi. The border was miles long and had no walls or guard. The barren region dissuaded most people from being in the area at all.

Tanner looked over to see that Palmer had noticed the vehicles as well. They were a pair of old Jeeps that had seen better days. Tanner and Palmer were riding in a Toyota Kluger that was a few years old but still in good shape.

When the Jeeps came closer, Tanner could see that there were three men riding in each of them. He had also noticed the barrel of a shotgun in the lead vehicle.

"That looks like trouble," Palmer said, as he grabbed up a walkie-talkie. "I'll call it in."

"I don't think there's time for that," Tanner told him. He brought the vehicle to a stop near a palm tree with a thick trunk after turning the Toyota sideways to the approaching Jeeps. Afterward, he stepped out to take a position behind the front end of the vehicle, where he could use the engine block for cover if needed. Palmer had released the walkie-talkie and followed suit.

The Jeeps slowed and came to a stop within speaking distance, and the men piled out of them. The driver of the first Jeep was a small dusky-skinned man with a trimmed beard that came to a point. He called to them in English.

"Are you two lost?"

"We're on patrol," Tanner said.

The man smiled. "You mean that you're lackeys for the general."

"And what are you and your friends?"

"We're businessmen. We make trades."

"What is it you trade?" Palmer asked.

"Right now, we're willing to trade you your lives for that Toyota."

Palmer cursed under his breath then spoke at a volume that only Tanner could hear.

"They're a bunch of rebels. They've taken over Dubabi and now they want to try their luck here."

"I'm going to kill them," Tanner said. "If we don't fight back, they'd kill us anyway."

"I'll take the guy with the shotgun; you kill the leader," Palmer said.

Tanner already liked Palmer. The man's lack of fear and willingness to fight against superior odds only made him like him more. Tanner unholstered his gun and fired in one smooth motion. His speed was such that most of the gang members only had time to twitch in reaction. The dusky man was the exception and had dropped down to take cover. Tanner had been aiming at the middle of the guy's chest. His round hit the man in the shoulder as he was ducking down. A second round caught another of the men in the neck. He had stood his ground and was bringing up his gun. He collapsed behind the Jeep amid a spray of blood.

Meanwhile, Palmer and the man with the shotgun had fired at each other. Palmer's round had hit home first, causing the shotgun wielder to jerk his weapon, sending shotgun pellets toward the sky. Palmer's aim had been good, and he had placed a bullet into his man's forehead.

The remaining shooters sent multiple rounds into the side of the Toyota. Windows shattered and one of the front tires went flat. The idiots had started the trouble while stating that they wanted to steal the vehicle, now they were destroying it.

Tanner and Palmer fired back with more discretion but were unable to hit anyone again.

"We need to make them defend themselves from two fronts," Tanner told Palmer. "I'm going to run for that palm tree and give them two targets to shoot at, it will also give me a better angle on them."

Palmer gave the tree a doubtful look. "That's nearly ten meters away and you'll be running on this sandy soil; you'd better move damn quick."

"Count on it."

Palmer told Tanner he would cover him while he made his sprint to the tree. They each had a limited number of rounds and such action would use up much of Palmer's ammo. They needed to end things before they found their guns empty.

"On three," Tanner said, then counted down. He rocketed out from behind their vehicle with his head down and his legs pumping. Palmer sent a steady stream of shots toward their enemies and kept them pinned down. As he neared the tree, from Tanner's left came the sound of the shotgun racking. Before the man holding it could fire, he screamed in pain as one of Palmer's rounds struck him in the side of the nose. The bullet obliterated his nostrils and the cartilage behind them. It wasn't a fatal injury, but it caused the man to drop the shotgun and fall to his knees screaming as blood poured from his wound.

From his new angle behind the tree, Tanner

could see the side of one of the men who had yet to be injured. He changed that by hitting him with two rounds.

Palmer cried out in pain. Tanner looked over to see that he was bleeding from the top of his left shoulder. He'd been nicked by a bullet fired by the dusky man.

"I'm all right!" Palmer called, then he held up three fingers. He was telling Tanner that he only had three rounds left. Tanner nodded his understanding as he reloaded his own weapon. They needed to finish this. He dropped flat at the base of the tree and gained a new perspective on the gang members. He was able to see the feet of a man who was firing at Palmer along with the knees of two men who were kneeling. Well placed rounds elicited screams as the men suffered wounds. Seeing an opening, Tanner left the cover of the tree and ran toward the enemy. As he reached the Jeep they were hiding behind, he propelled himself onto the hood.

The men crouched below him looked up with startled faces. Tanner shot them, his gun only inches away from their heads. The dusky man scrambled beneath the Jeep to get away. When he popped up from the other side Palmer was there and drilled him in the back.

Tanner slid off the Jeep and sent a mercy round into a man with ruined knees. It was the same man with the missing nose. The dusky man lived, although he would soon die. Palmer's shot had left him with a ragged exit wound to his gut. He was looking up at them while cursing in his native language between moans of agony. Palmer finished him off then looked back at their vehicle. It had two flat tires and was leaking fluid.

"I guess we'll have to ride back in one of their Jeeps."

A tinny-sounding voice was heard faintly. Someone was calling over the walkie-talkie. The din of the gun battle must have carried to the guards stationed along the wall at the pit where the palace was located.

Palmer took a step to answer it when Tanner asked him to wait for a moment.

"Wait for what?"

Tanner pointed at the dead men. "We have an opportunity here."

Palmer cocked his head. "Meaning?"

"We could report that these guys wanted to take our ride, or we can make it seem like more than it was. If we say that they admitted they were here to test the general's defenses, it will make what we did seem more important and get us noticed. I don't want to spend the rest of my time here riding around and looking at nothing. Maybe we can get moved to positions nearer the palace if we spin this right. It will mean a slight bump in pay too."

Palmer looked thoughtful for a few moments, then nodded. "It's worth a try and will make a name for us. Although, as bloody crazy as the general is, he might want to go to war with Dubabi."

"He tried that in the 1990s when there was a civil war and lost the land that Dubabi sits on. During that time was when he became desperate and started using children for soldiers. When a peace treaty was finally signed, sanctions were levied against Malika and the general was labeled a dictator."

Palmer nodded. "I don't like the man, but I need the money this gig pays."

"Same here," Tanner said.

The walkie-talkie squawked again. Palmer went over to grab it and smiled before pushing the talk button.

"Base. This is Palmer. We've had some serious trouble out here."

A voice answered. "What sort of trouble?"

"Someone was trying to attack the general."

THE LEADER OF THE GENERAL'S PERSONAL GUARD came out along with the regular guard supervisor and two of the guards who worked inside the palace.

The supervisor and the guards arrived in a vehicle. The leader of the elite guard was riding a horse.

Tanner's supervisor, Wes Walker, was more physically intimidating, but the head of the general's personal guard gave off an aura of danger despite his lean frame and average stature. His name was Jaheem. He had been forced to fight for the general when he was only eight-years-old. He had become a fierce soldier who had killed over a hundred men in combat. Jaheem was in his thirties and held the rank of colonel. He wore a green uniform and had a scar on his right cheek. His almond-shaped eyes were cold and glinted with high intelligence. Seated atop the horse he appeared majestic.

Walker, the supervisor of the guards, was dressed in a black suit and wore a matching hat with a wide brim. All the guards that worked in the palace wore black suits. Tanner figured that Walker wore the hat as a way to distinguish himself from his men. They all looked like secret service agents in the suits and talked to each other with two-way radios. Walker had the habit of chewing tobacco. There was always a wad of it wedged against his right cheek. The brand he preferred came in a package that was bright red with a green stripe.

Although he wasn't obvious about it, Tanner thought that Walker didn't like Westerners. It was the reason he had stuck himself and the Englishman

REMINGTON KANE

Palmer with the worst duty there was. The two of them had more experience in armed conflicts than most of the other men but that hadn't been recognized by Walker.

It was also rumored that Colonel Jaheem and Walker didn't get along. Walker resented the fact that he had no control over the colonel or his fellow ex-soldiers, while at the same time, the colonel could override Walker and give the guards he supervised assignments if he wanted to. That was the rumor, but the two men seemed civil enough to each other. Maybe the colonel resented Walker because the general had developed a fondness for the man and trusted him.

Despite his dislike of their backgrounds, Walker gave Tanner and Palmer a look of respect when he saw that they had killed six men. The only injury they suffered was the superficial wound to Palmer's left shoulder.

Colonel Jaheem displayed no emotion. He asked questions and listened as they were answered. Palmer was the target of his inquiries. When Palmer recounted how Tanner had charged toward the Jeep to leap onto its hood, the colonel shifted his eyes toward Tanner.

"Your actions were either brave or foolhardy. Which is it?"

"A little of both," Tanner said. "They had us

outnumbered and we were getting low on ammunition. Something needed to be done."

"And you did it," the colonel said.

Tanner told the lie about the dusky man mentioning that they were there to find out how tough the general's defenses were.

"He said that if we surrendered and cooperated that we wouldn't be tortured."

"He lied," the colonel said. "They would have taken you back to Dubabi and tortured you separately. If you both gave the same answers, then they would have known that you were telling the truth. After that, they would have killed you."

Walker, the supervisor, pointed down at the dead men. "This wasn't an act of war. I think they were going after Palmer and Foxx here in order to find out how difficult it would be to get to the general."

"As usual, you're stating the obvious, Walker," the colonel said, and Tanner saw irritation flash across Walker's face. It seemed that there was something to the rumor that the men disliked each other.

"Obvious or not, this is a problem. I'm going to double the patrol out here."

"Do that and you also double the chances of one of those patrols being captured. Instead, I'll have a temporary post setup that can keep an eye on the border. Instead of walkie-talkies we'll give them an alarm to sound off in case of trouble. If anyone attacks again, we'll send out a force to kill them."

"I guess that would work too," Walker said. "What we should do is lead a team of men into Dubabi and take the fight to them. If we hit those bastards hard enough, we might wipe them out."

"And we would also suffer losses that we can't afford, and possibly start a war. The palace might also be attacked while we were in Dubabi. I won't risk leaving the general unprotected."

"So instead we wait to be attacked again?"

Colonel Jaheem looked over at the bodies. "They may think twice before attempting that."

The colonel told Tanner and Palmer to ride back with Walker, and that the supervisor would drop them off at the barracks. Walker protested, saying that they would be needed to help dig graves for the dead men.

The colonel shook his head. "No graves. Have the bodies dumped along the border where they're likely to be found. That will let the thugs in charge of Dubabi know that they underestimated us."

"I could still use Palmer and Foxx to help with that."

"Summon others. It's work anyone can do. Not anyone could have defeated the odds they faced. I'll reward them by giving them the rest of the day off."

Walker put his fists on his hips. "They're my men, Colonel."

Colonel Jaheem's lips curled into a cruel smile. "And despite that, they performed well."

Walker stared at the colonel with malice in his eyes. After spitting out tobacco juice, he spoke. "Foxx, Palmer. When we return, head to the barracks and relax. The colonel is right; you've earned that much. But I'll want you ready for duty first thing tomorrow."

"Yes sir," Tanner answered along with Palmer.

IN THE MORNING, TANNER LEARNED THAT HE AND Palmer were being reassigned to one of the security booths that were positioned on the wall surrounding the old copper mine. He wondered if it was Walker's idea or the colonel's orders. He suspected it was the colonel.

From their new location, they overlooked the palace. It placed Tanner one step closer to the general. It was also better duty. The booth had power and could be temperature controlled.

Palmer sat in a swivel chair and smiled at Tanner. "This is nicer than riding around in the damn desert all day. And it upped our pay too."

Tanner nodded his agreement but wouldn't rest

until he wrangled his way into the palace. After witnessing the friction between the colonel and Walker, he had an idea that he might be able to use that hostility to his advantage. All he needed was a plan.

7

DISPOSING OF TRASH

WHEN TANNER WAS BEING BORED BY HIS PATROL duty, Soulless had been toiling in the mine. In order to extract the platinum, miners drilled holes and then packed them with explosives. The shattered rock was then collected, to later be transported to the surface. Soulless was assigned to a team that collected the rock. It was dirty, backbreaking work, but it gave him a reason to be in the mine. He was using the name Frank Brockton.

On his fourth day he was moving through an area where previous mining had been done. There was a sign written in several languages warning about the danger of entering a tunnel on their left. Soulless wondered for a moment why the men running the mine didn't just seal the tunnel off permanently, but then it hit him. The tunnel could be one of the possible escape routes that led to the underground entrance to the palace.

If it were sealed off, it would be that much harder for General Kwami to escape in case the palace was overrun.

Soulless memorized the way to the tunnel and would make it a point to return at another time. The mine was guarded when not in operation but was too big to keep watch over completely. It would be a thing of ease for him to sneak back into the mine over the weekend. The hard part would be reaching the area of the labyrinth that was beneath the general's palace.

Most of the men he worked with left him alone and he returned the favor. One man, a boisterous sort named Davies who told jokes, took a disliking to him. He was a white man from South Africa who had been designated to supervise Soulless's crew. If there was an unpleasant task or a particularly heavy chunk of rock to move, Davies always made sure that Soulless was chosen to deal with it.

Certain people had taken a disliking to Soulless his whole life, perhaps sensing that he was different. He wasn't like other people, didn't have their spectrum of emotions or sense of empathy.

When he'd first come across the term sociopath,

he looked up the definition. It stated that a sociopath was someone who was antisocial and couldn't understand the feelings of others. It also listed as traits the desire to control others and a willingness to adopt a charismatic or charming façade in order to get what they wanted.

Soulless didn't consider himself to be a sociopath. It was true that he could be labelled as antisocial, but he had no desire to control anyone and didn't go around trying to be charming unless he had to, like when he had charmed the lovely Heather. As for not understanding the emotions of others, that was nonsense. Soulless understood their emotions, he was just incapable of experiencing most of them. He didn't often feel anything other than the desire to complete a task, lust, and sometimes anger. He also enjoyed a challenge. Becoming an assassin was an ideal occupation for him. Killing was something he had done from a young age. It didn't thrill or repulse him but allowed him to make an excellent living without having to toil endlessly or work for someone else. Yes, he was different. But wasn't everyone different from everyone else?

Some who sensed his uniqueness were wise enough to steer clear of him, then there were the ones like Davies who wanted to upset him, as they tried to provoke a reaction and shatter his stoic demeanor. Davies was a problem because he had a modicum of authority at the mine and might cause Soulless to lose his job. Soulless needed to remain at the mine. He didn't need Davies to go on breathing. Soulless didn't react or complain about the treatment Davies gave him. He would handle Davies away from the mine. Come Monday morning, he and the others in his crew would need to be assigned a new supervisor.

REGINALD DAVIES DIDN'T LIKE SOULLESS. IT WASN'T because he sensed his dark nature or lack of empathy. No, it was far simpler than that. The man never laughed at his jokes.

Davies prided himself on his ability to make people laugh. The rest of the men he supervised thought he was a fine fellow and found him to be humorous and a good storyteller. Davies believed that it made the time pass more quickly if everyone was in a good mood.

One of the new men, a lowly laborer, Frank Brockton, never laughed. He never smiled, nor did he frown. Davies had met men like him before. They were humorless jerks who went through life with a sour disposition. Unable to make them laugh, he would try to elicit other reactions out of them, such as anger.

He was a big man, had been a fighter when younger, and didn't fear getting into a brawl. If a man wouldn't laugh at his jokes, he'd get back at them when the chance arose. Since he was Brockton's supervisor, the opportunities to do so were frequent, but the son of a bitch never took the bait. He never got angry, showed impatience, or complained. It just pissed Davies off all the more. The next time something went wrong in the mine, he would find a way to blame Brockton for it and get the man fired. Hell, screwups happened all the time. Maybe then he'd see some emotion from Frank Brockton.

THE WEEKEND FOUND DAVIES AT A BAR IN THE CITY of Yousho. Like the rest of Malika, it was second-rate at best, but there was nightlife and the younger generation it attracted weren't as careworn as their parents. They hadn't lived through the war years and General Kwami had become less controlling of the people's everyday lives as he aged. There was a time when the general would issue a new dictate every week. They concerned everything from how late people were allowed on the roads to the colors that were acceptable to use as paint for one's home or automobile. The authoritarian bastard had either stopped caring about such trivial matters or old age had mellowed him. Either way, the city was on the cusp of a renaissance as old buildings were refurbished and trade was expanding over the internet. Most of this was due to the influence of the general's young son, nicknamed Prince. In the last few years, work visas had been granted as foreign workers were needed to fill jobs in a burgeoning tech sector. The city of Yousho's rebirth had attracted young people from other countries, most notably Davies's native South Africa.

Davies was always on the lookout for attractive women, and each conquest became a new story for his repertoire.

THE BAR DAVIES WAS IN WAS ONE HE OFTEN mentioned when telling his stories. He'd sent drinks to a table where two white women were seated and was rewarded with smiles after they had both looked him over. Their names were Haley and Page. Page was married to a native of the country and the mother of two young children, but Haley, a blonde with green eyes, was newly divorced and worked as a nurse. She and Page had been friends since grade school.

Davies had them laughing within a minute and charmed them with his stories about his former life in the navy. After the third drink, Page said she had to get home. Haley stayed and Davies was certain he would be getting lucky. He left the bar with Haley around midnight and they took a cab to her apartment. He never noticed the old car that was following them.

HALEY WAS GIGGLING AT SOMETHING DAVIES SAID AS she opened the door to her loft. After riding the elevator up to her floor, they had stood outside her apartment kissing. They were on the fifth floor of an apartment building that catered to young singles. The building had once been a warehouse where the general had stored the weapons he'd bought on the black-market. Several of his enemies had been tortured in its basement. That was all decades ago. No one living in the building had a clue about its dark history. The building was quiet, and few lights shone in windows. Most of Haley's neighbors were either asleep or out on the town themselves on a Friday night.

Davies never heard the person coming up behind

him until it was too late. As a gloved hand was clamped over his mouth, a fist flew past his head and struck Haley with a brutal blow to the side of her head. She had been turning to say something and took the hard punch to her temple. She collapsed in the doorway, where she moaned. The same fist that struck her moved backwards and hit Davies in the throat. He gasped beneath the hand still clamped over his mouth as panic alighted in his eyes. He was having trouble breathing.

He gulped in air as the hand was removed from his mouth. A hard shove sent him stumbling forward and he tripped over Haley.

Haley was recovering from the blow she'd received although her eyes were still closed. It was for the best. If she'd seen the masked man leaning over her, she would have only been terrified. It would have also necessitated a change of plans that would have ended with her death. Instead, she was rendered unconscious by a swift kick that rocked her head. She had never seen the masked man, and so she would live.

Davies was getting his breath back. He stood on a pair of shaky legs as he raised his hands to defend himself. He hadn't had a boxing match in over thirteen years and he'd also been fitter and thinner then. Even at his prime he'd had a losing record.

The masked man sent a kick into his knee that

hurt like hell. As Davies opened his mouth to scream a fist mashed his lips and stifled the sound. Then came another blow to his head and Davies tripped and fell onto a sofa. The masked man moved in and rained hard punches on Davies, rendering him senseless.

SOULLESS GAVE DAVIES ONE FINAL PUNCH WITH A gloved hand, then stood and listened. None of Haley's neighbors opened their doors to investigate the sounds of struggle and there were no shouts of alarm. His assault hadn't been silent, but he had managed to keep his victims from crying out.

After dragging Haley out of the threshold, Soulless shut the door and locked it. He'd had to remove Haley's keys, as they had still been in the lock. He checked on Haley and determined that she would be out for a while.

A look around the loft apartment revealed that Haley was a fan of abstract paintings. They hung on walls of sand-blasted brick and filled the room with color. Soulless liked art, but his tastes ran to sculpture. He was especially fond of Michelangelo's masterpieces.

Once he had stripped a pillowcase off the bed, he used it to gather up Haley's purse, jewelry, laptop, and a camera. Now came the hard part. He had to move Davies downstairs. Fortunately, there was an elevator. Soulless loaded Davies's limp form onto his shoulder in a fireman carry. He'd always been strong, and Davies's two hundred and five pounds was manageable.

Haley's apartment door was left sitting open as he trudged over to the elevator. It was still on the fifth floor, so the doors opened up right away. The elevator came to a jarring stop at the bottom of the ride, and with Davies weight on him, Soulless's knees nearly buckled.

Soulless had his gun out and was ready to kill any witnesses. The doors opened in the lobby to reveal no one; however, there was the sound of a car braking out front, it was followed by voices.

Soulless moved down a tiled corridor and ducked into a slanted alcove that was formed by the rise of the staircase. There was a bike under there with a wheel missing. On the floor beside it was a discarded candy wrapper.

The apartment house door opened, and the voices grew more distinct. They were talking loudly; the way people do when they're drunk. One voice was female, the other a guy's voice. It looked as if Haley wasn't the only one to bring a drinking companion home.

They were barely on the elevator when Soulless

left the alcove and continued along the corridor until he reached the rear of the building. Davies's bulk was becoming a burden that Soulless was looking forward to shedding.

Soulless turned the knobs on two deadbolts and opened a steel door to find a wooden platform. A whooshing sound came from the left. Soulless turned his head in that direction and saw a bag of garbage leave a chute and drop inside a large dumpster. It gave him an idea.

Davies was deposited onto the platform with a thud. Freeing himself of the man's weight felt wonderful to Soulless. It was now time to free himself of the man completely. He had been intending to toss Davies into the trunk of the car he'd stolen and dispose of the body somewhere. The apartment house dumpster seemed as good a place as any.

He removed his mask and felt the cool night air caress his face. The mask had been hot and there was a sheen of perspiration on his brow.

"Brockton?"

That whispered word came from Davies. He had regained consciousness but was still too stunned to make it to his feet. Soulless gazed at him without expression. It was time to finish things.

Soulless raised his foot and brought it down with force on Davies's throat. A croaking sound was heard, and the man's eyes bulged in their sockets. Davies's hands grabbed onto Soulless's leg, but he was unable to prevent Soulless from raising his foot again. He stamped hard on his supervisor's throat two more times. The final blow broke something in Davies's neck. His arms fell to his sides as his head lolled at an odd angle. The man's eyes remained open, but they no longer saw anything.

Once again Davies was lifted up, this time to be tossed into the dumpster. The weight of the body pushed it past the sacks of refuse and out of sight.

Haley would recover her senses at some point and awaken to find her valuables missing. Her last conscious thought would be of opening her apartment door to the guy she had met in the bar. Davies had used his credit card to buy drinks. It wouldn't take long for the cops to name Davies as Haley's assailant. He would go missing and assumed to be on the run.

If Davies's body surfaced instead of winding up at a landfill to rot for eternity, he would then be categorized as another victim in the case. Either way, he wouldn't be coming back to the mine and there was nothing to connect Soulless's phony identity to any of it.

Soulless returned to his stolen vehicle and pointed it in the direction of the mine. He was going there to do some off-hours exploring. If he was very lucky, he'd stumble across General Kwami's secret exit from the palace. He didn't need such luck. His plan only required that he find a path to the area beneath the palace. Once he had that route mapped out, the general would be mere days away from dying.

8

TIME OFF

BEING REASSIGNED TO ONE OF THE SECURITY BOOTHS that were positioned on the rim of the old copper mine had gotten Tanner closer to his target, but not close enough. He needed to move things along.

He'd completed his first two weeks of duty and received the promised day off. He and Palmer, along with the other five men they'd been hired with, were dropped off in the city of Yousho. It was evening and they were told to report to the drop-off point twenty-four hours later when the van would return with a different group of guards.

Four of the men went to a nearby bar with plans to visit a brothel afterwards, another man, Younger, said he had a woman waiting for him at a restaurant. While they'd been allowed to have beer with their evening meal at the compound, hard liquor was

107

forbidden, and there were no women at the compound other than several older ladies who cooked the meals and cleaned.

Upon their arrival in town, Palmer told Tanner that he would see him the next day. He took off walking as if he were familiar with the city and had a definite destination in mind.

Tanner didn't know where his colleague was headed and didn't care. He was glad he wouldn't have to come up with an excuse to separate from him and possibly cause Palmer to wonder where he'd gone. Tanner walked three blocks in the opposite direction that Palmer had taken and entered a small hotel.

After checking in for the night he used the phone in his room to call a number he'd memorized. When his call was answered by an efficient female voice, he said his assumed name.

"This is Brett Foxx. Are there any messages for me?"

There was a slight pause before the woman responded. "No messages, sir. Can I help you with anything else?"

"No. That will be all."

"Goodbye then."

There was a click on the line as if his party had hung up. If the line were tapped the innocuous conversation would have been the only thing recorded. The woman who answered was a United States government agent and an expert in communication equipment. Tanner's call had been switched to an encrypted line impossible to trace. Tanner kept the phone to his ear and waited. His end of the brief conversation had signaled to the agent that he wanted to call home. There was the sound of a phone ringing a few seconds later. It was answered in the middle of the second ring.

"Hello?"

Tanner smiled as he heard Sara's voice. "It's me. How is everything there?"

"We're good, but we all miss you so much."

"I've missed all of you too."

"How are you doing?"

"I'm working as a guard for the general, but I've yet to lay eyes on him."

He heard a faint sigh as Sara spoke. "I guess that means you'll be gone longer?"

"Yes. But I have no plans to make a career out of this. I'll find a way to carry out the contract and get back home as soon as possible."

"I know you will. Hold on. Someone wants to talk to you."

Tanner heard the phone being passed, then the sound of his son's voice.

"Hi, Daddy."

A grin lit Tanner's face as he spoke. "Hi, buddy. I've missed you, Lucas."

"I've missed you too, and Daddy?"

"Yes, buddy?"

"I've been doing what you said. I'm looking out for Mommy and Marian and being good."

"That's my boy. I'm sure that Mommy appreciates it."

"When are you coming home?"

"I don't know yet, but I'll try to make it soon."

"I love you, Daddy."

"I love you too, Lucas."

Sara came back on the line. "He misses you so much; we all do."

"You know that I'll get back to you as soon as I can."

"I know, but don't take too many chances. I can only imagine how hard it will be to kill the general and still be able to escape."

"The escape will be the easy part once I reach the rendezvous point. Lawson has people standing by to get me out of the country."

"What is it like there? Is it dangerous?"

"We had a run-in with a group of thugs and dealt with it."

"We?"

"I've been partnered up with a guy named Colin Palmer. He handles himself well."

"Please be careful. No. On second thought, just be yourself. That will mean you'll be fine."

"I've made some progress, but I've yet to think of a way to get close to the general."

"You'll think of something; you always do. What's the weather like there? Is it very hot?"

"It's similar to Texas this time of year, maybe a little less humid, and the nights are cooler."

"That's good. I thought you might be living in desert conditions."

They talked a little longer before ending the call. Tanner lay back on his bed and stared up at the ceiling. He had to come up with a plan that would put him within reach of the general.

He thought of a strategy he could use an hour later. It involved risk, but that was a given anyway. The greater the risk, the greater the reward. He left the hotel and went for a walk. Moving would help him think better and refine his idea. A light rain began to fall. It was the first precipitation he'd seen since entering the region. It felt refreshing and he moved along faster, then broke into a run.

As his arms and legs pumped and he propelled himself along, the plan he'd come up with gained greater detail, even as his desire to kill the general increased. The sooner he killed the general, the quicker he'd be back home with his family. The man couldn't die soon enough.

Soulless parked his stolen vehicle behind a small hill and made his way on foot to the mine. It was over a mile away and he wore a backpack that he'd bought before tracking Davies down at the bar. It was necessary to approach quietly. Sound carried easily in the area and he didn't want the guard to hear the car's engine. Rain was moving in from the southeast but not a drop had yet to fall near the mine. Still, clouds were gathering, and he had to walk slowly as the moonlight faded.

There was nothing near the mine and no reason for anyone to be driving around the area at night. Hearing the car would have only placed the gate guard on alert. The guard shack was below the rim of the pit that had been dug out long ago by copper miners. There were fences with locked gates to either side of the shack. The left gate was for traffic exiting the pit, while the right side was for vehicles venturing into the manmade canyon. The roads had been carved out of the pit's walls. To get to the bottom of the pit where the entrance to the platinum mine was, you had to drive in a zig-zag pattern and navigate more than a dozen turns. It took time to reach the bottom and the going was slow because the incline of each level was mild. The giant vehicles named haul trucks used the road to ferry rock to a nearby processing plant. When loaded, the monster-sized trucks weighed over two hundred tons. It wouldn't be a good idea to have such vehicles climbing up and down steep hills.

Soulless used a cheap pair of binoculars to spy on the guard from the edge of the rim. It was an old man. He was seated on a stool and looking through a newspaper as a radio played marabi music. Given the volume of the music, Soulless knew he could have risked driving closer. He scanned the pit itself and saw that all was quiet. The office trailer was dark, and the haul trucks were idle but were positioned beneath the conveyer belts that would fill them with fresh stone after the weekend.

There was a scent of water in the air that had nothing to do with the impending rain. A lake was up a nearby hill and above the level of the mine. If it had been in a less desolate area, homes might have been built around it.

Miles to the west was the general's palace. The dictator's home was at the bottom of a different pit that was just as deep but far wider. Soulless was betting that he could find the tunnel that connected the two sites. His plan depended on it.

He looked at the guard shack again. *One lone sentry.* It was not surprising. What was there to steal? Any would-be thieves would have to have a knowledge of explosives and be willing to put in hours of hard work to even have a hope of extracting platinum from the mine. For each ounce of platinum tons of rock had to be removed. Not an easy task, and one that needed a lot of workers to get it done. And as for the cheap furniture and computers in the office trailer, well, there were closer places to town where one could steal such things.

The guard shack faced away from the mine and was high above it. Given that the rickety mine elevator was recessed, Soulless doubted the old guard would hear it operating from his shack. Especially if he kept the radio on. Another source of noise would be the ventilation fans. Air had to be drawn in and circulated throughout the mine to maintain a healthy level of oxygen. As noisy as the system was, it was located deep in the mine. No one should be able to hear it running from the outside.

Soulless used a screwdriver to remove the front panel on the elevator's controls. He was in the smaller elevator used for inspections. The main elevator was enormous and could hold over a hundred men. It also made more noise.

Once Soulless had the panel off, he manipulated wires to get the elevator to run. It was similar to hotwiring an old car. When he was finished, he'd screw the front plate back on and no one would be the wiser. That is, until someone performed routine maintenance on the machine. From what Soulless had seen of working conditions. The elevator wouldn't be serviced unless it broke and needed repair.

He took it down to the level where he'd seen the warning signs posted across the tunnel entrance. There was a headlamp strapped to his forehead that gave off good light. In the backpack he wore, Soulless carried extra batteries for it, along with food, water, rope, a blanket, and moist towelettes.

His plan was to spend the better part of the weekend exploring the old mine shafts. Thanks to his familiarity with the mine, he knew his way around and was knowledgeable about its systems. Had he simply snuck into the mine without having first worked there, he'd have had no idea of where to start and would have wasted time wandering. There would be enough of that as it were.

The blanket he carried with him could act as a thin mattress when he napped while also providing warmth. In his pocket he had a compact notepad along with a compass and sticks of chalk. He would draw a crude map and jot down anything of note. With the chalk he could leave behind marks, so he'd know if he'd already been down a passageway. The last thing he wanted was to become lost in the maze of crude pathways.

If he could locate General Kwami's escape

tunnel he could be certain that he was directly beneath the palace. That would be a best-case scenario. What would be acceptable is assurance that he had located the overall region beneath the palace. Once he found a pathway to that area, he'd be halfway home.

There was also his escape to plan, but he had an idea how to accomplish that. If he timed things right, he could hitch a ride on the freight train that moved through the area. It ran on time most days and traveled at a steady but slow speed. He still had his motorcycle. He could catch up to the train within minutes and get onto it. He'd be out of Malika and headed to safety before the authorities could get themselves together. Besides, he would give them plenty of other things to occupy them.

It felt pleasing to be alone and away from the mindless chatter of other people. The average person spent a large chunk of their lives obsessed with petty or meaningless activities, such as watching sports or movies and TV. Those were things Soulless rarely did. And once watched, he certainly didn't feel the need to discuss them with others. His fellow miners could be heard going on and on about a disputed call made by a referee during a game. They also disparaged any player who had failed to perform well, as if the man lost the match on purpose. If placed on the soccer field, the armchair critics would be hopelessly outclassed by the other players and embarrass themselves.

Anyway, what did it matter who won a game or lost? They were games, singular events staged as entertainment. If they spent half of that attention and passion on improving their own lives, they would be much better off. Instead, they would toil in the mine or work other hard and dirty jobs until they were too old or too beaten down by life to do so anymore. Then they retire in poverty and continue to watch younger, more talented men play games on TV. When they die, it will be a relief for them because it will end the tedium of their lives.

Soulless couldn't imagine living such an existence. He had always been willing to risk himself in order to better his place in life. He never lost sight of the fact that he would die someday, and that there was no way to be safe. If safety was an impossibility and the afterlife an unknown, why not live life one's own way and go after what you wanted?

Soulless wanted to be the greatest assassin of all time. If he lived long enough, he knew he would make it. Once he reached that pinnacle, he'd surpass himself and continue to kill difficult targets like the general.

Someday, when he had enough money to carry him into a comfortable old age, he'd choose the targets himself. Killing was something he figured he'd always do and dealing with clients only increased the risk that the authorities might track him down. No clients, less risk, and there was no shortage of self-important people who he'd like to put in the ground.

After eating an energy bar, Soulless began his trek among the old tunnels. It was dark, silent, and dangerous. Soulless felt right at home.

9

ETERNAL NIGHT

TANNER'S RUN IN THE SOFT EVENING RAIN HAD TAKEN him to the bar where his fellow guards were hanging out. He'd yet to have a drink while they were all feeling no pain. He bought a round for the table and listened to their inebriated patter.

A beautiful young woman with skin the color of mochaccino was seated alone at the bar. She'd shot down several men who'd bought her drinks but was giving Tanner looks that signaled he might have more success. When the other men rose to head to the brothel, Tanner nodded in the direction of the woman and told the men that he would try his luck with her. The men laughed, wished him happy hunting, and went off to where they were guaranteed a sure thing, for a price.

Tanner had no intention of having a one-night

stand. Showing interest in the woman had made a handy excuse for him to beg off a trip to the brothel with the others. He wanted his fellow guards to see him as just another guy. If he acted in ways they expected, then he wouldn't stand out or arouse suspicion.

He moved over to the bar but sat several stools away from the woman. She gave him a sideways glance and he sent her a nod. Before marrying Sara, he'd have been all over her and ready to take her back to his room. When he made no move to talk to her, she turned her attention to a dark-skinned man wearing a good suit. When the guy walked over and sat beside her, they seemed to get along well.

You snooze, you lose, Tanner thought, and ordered another drink. He was finishing the drink and thinking of returning to the hotel when Palmer entered the bar. Tanner waved him over then gestured for the bartender, signaling that he would buy Palmer a drink while having another one himself.

As Palmer settled on a stool beside him, Tanner studied him. The man's eyes were red, as if he'd been crying. When the drinks came, Palmer thanked Tanner before downing the whiskey in a series of gulps. Afterward, he ordered another and one for Tanner. Tanner had yet to take a sip of his third drink. He swiveled around to face Palmer and asked a question.

"What's wrong?"

"What do you mean?"

"We've spent most of the last two weeks together. I can tell when something is bothering you."

Palmer's fresh drink came. He swallowed a gulp, sighed, then glanced at Tanner.

"It's my wife. She's sick and needs an operation. She's on the list for treatment, but her name is so far down the bloody queue that she'll be dead before they get to her."

"Is that why you're here in Africa? To make enough money to get her treatment elsewhere?"

Palmer nodded. "This gig pays well, but it won't be enough, and in the meantime I'm away from my wife."

Tanner could understand the man's situation. Palmer wanted to help his wife, but by doing so he was leaving her alone when she needed him the most.

Palmer released a long sigh. "I'm thinking of leaving Malika and finding another way to get the money. The only thing wrong with that idea is that I don't know what else I could do. I'm no damn bank robber. I wish those arseholes wc killed the other day had been a serious threat against the general. By stopping them, we would have been in line for a huge reward. That's what I want, a chance to stop an assassin. The general would make me a wealthy man then."

"That he would," Tanner said. He'd been glad to be teamed up with Palmer. Now, he knew the man had every reason to want to see his head on a platter.

Tanner picked up his drink and took a sip. It would be best if Palmer did decide to leave Malika. He would hate to have to kill the man if he got between him and the fulfilling of a contract.

Palmer looked at Tanner. "Why are you hanging out in this bar? I'd thought you'd be at the whorehouse with the others."

"I tried to get lucky here but struck out. Now, I think I just want to get some sleep."

"You've gotten a hotel room?"

"Yeah."

"Me too, and I'm looking forward to a good night's sleep. Those cots back at the barracks are like sleeping on the ground, and that bloke Younger snores like a chainsaw."

"Where is your wife, back in England?"

"Yeah," Palmer said. "My mum's looking after her." He shook his head. "I should be there."

Tanner knew the feeling. He wished he was at home too.

~

SOULLESS EXPLORED THE TUNNELS IN THE MINE IN A methodical manner. From having worked in them the week before, he knew that time passed differently far below ground. Twenty minutes could seem like two or feel like fifty. The constant chill in the air took some getting used to as well.

He was making good progress in charting the tunnels but had wound up at numerous dead-ends. The old man, Teesoo, had spoken of tunnels that led nowhere. What he hadn't mentioned was the tunnels that looped around in a crude circle. Twice, Soulless had ventured through long passages only to find himself back in the cavern where he'd begun. If he hadn't used the chalk to mark the walls, he might have spent hours repeating the same path. He was looking for a long passageway that would take him to the area directly below the general's palace, or a series of tunnels that would do the same thing. If it led him to the very spot that the general would use to make an escape, so much the better.

He'd yet to find such a tunnel after hours of effort, but he was determined to do so. A check of the compass assured him that he was traveling in the right direction and not being led in a circle. Ten minutes later he came to another dead-end and had to turn around.

As he trudged back the way he had just come a revelation struck him. The palace was miles away.

Considering that, and the general's age, Soulless thought that wherever the general's escape route was located, there would be a way for him to move along it without having to slog about on foot.

"Tracks," Soulless whispered. There would be tracks laid in the correct tunnel. Light railing and some sort of conveyance to travel along it, like a handcar that could be pumped to make it move. The more he considered it, the surer Soulless was convinced that he was right. If he found a set of well-maintained tracks inside one of the older tunnels, it would be a sign that he was closing in on the general's escape route. In the meantime, Soulless continued his exploration underground in darkness that was like an eternal night.

MERCY

THE BED IN TANNER'S HOTEL ROOM WAS comfortable; however, he abandoned it in the early morning hours. The plan he'd come up with required him to make a trip across the border and into Dubabi. The rain had stopped, and the moon was again bright overhead. That was good. He would need the moonlight to see by later on.

There was no shortage of old cars in Malika and without modern theft deterrents they were all easy to steal.

Crossing over the Dubabi border wasn't difficult, as there were no checkpoints or barriers. The general's edict about shooting illegal immigrants dissuaded all but the bold from traveling south into Malika, while no one from Malika would want to enter the zone of chaos Dubabi had become.

Tanner rode along streets that hadn't seen a road repair crew in years. Potholes were the norm and the buildings lining the streets were just as decrepit. Say what you would about General Kwami, but the streets in Malika were passable.

Many of the buildings in Dubabi had been recent victims of fire and Tanner had spotted more than one that was marred by dozens of bullet holes. Leadership of the country had changed hands frequently in recent years and was currently controlled by thugs who called themselves rebels. They had attained power but knew nothing about governing. It was just a matter of time until another faction opposed them, which would bring more misery to Dubabi's citizens.

Tanner stuck out as a white man. By being inside a car he reduced his chances of being seen. The fact that it was the middle of the night meant less people were around. However, the people he was looking for would be awake. They were the type who preferred to operate outside of daylight hours.

He heard the music first then saw the lit up storefront from two blocks away. He pulled the car over and parked to get a better look. Tanner had a cheap pair of plastic binoculars that he'd bought at a convenience store in Malika. They weren't much more than a toy but did magnify things somewhat.

The well-lit storefront was a restaurant that sold

Kati Kati. Kati Kati was a type of spicy chicken popular in Africa. Tanner could smell the food from where he was two blocks away and it stirred his appetite. Several men were seated out front at tables. They were rebels. They openly carried rifles and had the look of thugs. They were who Tanner was looking for.

HE LEFT THE CAR AND APPROACHED THE RESTAURANT by circling around to the rear of the building. The music was loud, blasting, and he had to rely on sight to tell if anyone was around him. Someone could have approached from behind while snapping their fingers and not been heard over the music.

There was a parking lot beside the restaurant. Tanner waited there in the shadows, with his back against a wall. He was unarmed except for a knife. It was rare for him to be without a firearm, but he would correct that as soon as he could. The opportunity arrived when one of the gang members stumbled into view. Along with food, the restaurant sold liquor, and the guy was drunk.

Tanner came up behind him as he was opening a car door to get in. He had a knife at the ready although he didn't want to use it unless he had to. He needed to leave one man alive; it might as well be the drunk. He struck the man on the side of the head with an elbow, then kicked him on the chin after he'd dropped to the ground. Along with the rifle the guy also had a gun strapped on his hip. It was a Vektor CP1. Tanner had seen a Vector years ago when he'd been in Australia and thought it had minor flaws, such as the rear sights being made of plastic. The drunk at his feet hadn't kept the weapon in pristine condition but it would work if fired. The rifle was a variant of an AK-47.

After checking the man for another weapon, he left something in the punk's front pocket. Afterward, Tanner dragged the drunk away from the car. On the rear seat was an old cigar box. When Tanner looked inside, he found extra ammunition for both weapons. He tucked the spare magazines into his pockets and headed out to the street. He wore a cap on his head with the bill pulled down low to place his eyes in shadow. His eyes were memorable, and he didn't want to risk being identified later.

Five more gang members were seated in front of the restaurant. Three were at one table and two at another. The three were all busy eating with their heads down. The two seated together were involved in a conversation and having drinks. How they could hear each other over the music was a mystery to Tanner. A rock song was blasting out of the speaker fastened over the restaurant's door. The rebels' rifles were either leaning against the back of their chairs or lying flat on the ground. Tanner used his rifle to destroy the speaker and the music ceased. The five men looked startled by the sound of the shot and the ensuing silence it caused. When they spotted Tanner, the men's eyes widened. He spoke to them in English.

"I was going to kill you, but maybe I won't have to. Slide those rifles over here."

One of the men said something that might have been a curse. His mouth was so full of chicken that Tanner couldn't understand him. He was able to discern his belligerent tone, and when the man grabbed his rifle, Tanner shot him.

The other four went for their guns as well. Tanner shot two more of them. As he was taking aim at a fourth man, he realized that the fifth man had been faster and already had his rifle shouldered. Tanner dropped to the ground, as he did so, he released the rifle and brought out the handgun. Rounds flew over his head as the pistol barked. It killed the man who had fired at him and wounded his slower companion with a bullet to the face that had struck him sideways. The man's cheeks were bloody, and bits of broken teeth fell from his mouth as he howled in pain.

Meanwhile, one of the men Tanner had shot earlier was back in the fight even though he had two wounds to his chest. Whether it was the pain of his wounds or just bad aim, his shots were wide and too high. Tanner killed him with a shot to the head as he made it back to his feet, then he killed the man he had wounded in the face.

One of the other gang members was still alive but wouldn't be for long. He'd suffered two rounds to the abdomen and was lying in a pool of blood. Along with his rifle he had a gun in a holster. It was a .45 revolver. After claiming the thug's gun, Tanner reached into a pocket and took out a folded piece of material that was green with black and yellow stripes. It was a Malikan flag. He dropped it on top of one of the bodies.

Tanner ran into the parking lot, climbed a fence, and soon made it back to his stolen car. He drove with his headlights off. When he was several blocks away from the scene, he saw three cars speeding toward him in the distance. He pulled to the curb and parked. The cars grew closer. There were four of them. Another car had turned off a side street and joined the pack.

Tanner slid down in the seat until his head was below the level of the windows. The cars flew past. They were no doubt more rebels. A worker in the restaurant must have made a call and the troops were being rallied. It wouldn't be long until they were out for blood. Leaving the flag behind signaled to them who their enemy was. Along with the six men whose corpses had been dumped on the Dubabi doorstep days earlier, the thugs would believe that the general was looking for a fight.

Tanner crossed over the border and drove his stolen vehicle toward the general's compound. He had more trouble to stir up. So much for relaxing on his day off.

COLONEL JAHEEM HAD SET UP A TEMPORARY OUTPOST near the border after Tanner and Palmer had dispatched the rebels in the Jeeps days earlier.

At night, the outpost stood out like a beacon in the darkness. It was just an old office trailer that had once been used on construction sites. It had a compost toilet and a water tank. Power was supplied by a solar generator that was connected to the photovoltaic panels on the trailer's roof. There were two men stationed in the trailer at all times. They kept watch over a set of cameras that had night vision capability. If anything approached from the Dubabi side of the border they were to use a siren to sound an alarm.

Tanner had seen the flaw right away and took advantage of it. He crossed over the border beyond the range of the cameras. The area was steep and rocky. Climbing it at night was treacherous and he had to take his time. Had he not been in excellent condition and had experience rock climbing, the ascent would have been almost impossible in the dark.

Once across the border, Tanner walked into Malika until he was even with the outpost but east of it. He then approached the trailer from behind and moved around it silently until he was at the front of it. He pressed his body against the structure's metal surface. The cameras were above his head; there were three of them. If he moved too far away from the trailer or attempted to enter it through the door at its front, he would be captured on video.

There was a gap at the edge of the window blinds that allowed him to see inside. He was disheartened to realize that he recognized the two men on duty. Their names were Gregor and Howard. Although he was only pretending to be a guard to get close to the general in order to murder him, it would still feel treacherous to kill men that he knew and who considered him a colleague. He'd known when he'd chosen this course of action to infiltrate the guards that it was something he would no doubt have to do. Other people would have to die if he were to assassinate General Kwami, but he was not looking forward to killing men he had lived alongside of for weeks.

The two in the trailer would die tonight. They had signed on with the general knowing it was a possibility. Tanner still felt a twist in his gut as he took aim through the window with the .45 he'd acquired in Dubabi. He had eaten with Gregor and Howard in the mess tent, and they slept in the same barracks with him.

He lowered his weapon a few seconds later and stuck it in his belt. He would make a change to the plan. Tanner aimed the rifle upward and destroyed the cameras with three shots. More shots from the automatic, the Vector, damaged the floodlights illuminating the area in front of the trailer. He then fired into the trailer itself with the revolver, being careful to aim high. Next, he blew out the windows of the trailer. They shattered with a cacophonous noise that competed with the sound of the gun.

Tanner could hear Gregor swearing in Russian as he and Howard dived to the floor. He moved away from them while running. At his back, someone sent three shots through the door as a warning to their attackers to stay outside.

Tanner was a quarter of a mile away and headed back the way he'd come when the alarm sounded. He couldn't imagine it was needed. The gunfire had to have been heard by others. More guards would soon be headed to the area. They would begin a search and be ready to kill anyone they came across.

By the time Tanner reached the base of the rocky ridge the landscape behind him was filled with searchlights as vehicles moved about looking for him. They were still focused on the area directly in front of the trailer and had yet to expand the search.

He was cresting the rock when he heard a barrage of gunfire. He was too far away for a rifle round to reach him but ducked down instinctively as he spun to look behind him. Someone, perhaps the colonel, had given the order for the men to line up and shoot into the darkness. If anyone was in the path of the bullets they would be wounded, if not slain outright.

Tanner returned to his stolen vehicle and drove back to Yousho. He had used three weapons during his assault on the trailer. All three weapons used different ammunition. Shell casings would distinguish the Vector's rounds from those of the AK-47. As for the .45, the holes in the trailer would speak for themselves. It might lead to a conclusion that there had been more than one shooter.

The gang running Dubabi would believe that they'd been attacked by the general's men, while Colonel Jaheem would assume that the rebels had made an attempt at payback for the six men who had died the week before. Tension would be in the air and a fire started. When it came to a head and the general's security was occupied, Tanner would use that opportunity to go after the man. The odds would still be stacked against him, but he was someone well-accustomed to overcoming tremendous opposition. He also had an ace up his sleeve. If played right, it could win him the game.

Tanner returned the stolen car where he'd found it. Not only was it still in good shape, but Tanner had filled its tank. A twenty-minute walk saw him back at the hotel as the sun was just peaking over the horizon. After a shower, Tanner tumbled into bed and was asleep in less than a minute. When he dreamt, he dreamed of returning home. It was a vision he was determined to make a reality as soon as possible.

11

THE NEEDLE IN THE HAYSTACK

SOULLESS HAD SEEN DAYBREAK ARRIVE FROM THE entrance to the mine. He'd come up to make sure that the guard hadn't detected his presence. All was well, and he went back into the earth where he settled down on his blanket for a few hours of sleep.

He dreamt every night but seldom retained any recall of them. The ones he did remember were more like distorted memories of his past in Russia.

Soulless didn't like thinking about the past. He lived his life going forward and always had a goal to drive him. He'd been that way even as a boy.

He'd been small for his age when he was younger. Combined with his natural taciturn nature, he was a prime target for a bully. Soulless's bully had been a boy named Ivan who was older and much bigger than he was. Ivan and his family lived near Soulless's family and Soulless found himself encountering Ivan often. He never ran away from the boy, had tried to fight back, but was too small and had no skills at the time to overcome the physical disadvantage. What Soulless did have was an imagination. He often imagined what life would be like if Ivan were no longer around. Whenever he visualized that, a smile brightened his face. The desire strengthened and gave birth to a plan, a way to make certain that Ivan never bullied him again.

Ivan was a sleepwalker. The boy had once been found blocks away from his home in the middle of the night dressed in his underwear. When he was returned home, the front door was found sitting open with Ivan's parents blissfully asleep and unaware of their son's nocturnal stroll.

It happened once more, and Soulless saw no reason why it couldn't happen again. Not far away from where they lived was a steep hill with rocks at its base. Young Soulless's plan involved guiding a sleepwalking Ivan right off the edge of that hill. Everyone would think it to be an accident and a bully would be dead.

He spent weeks waking up at two a.m. with the help of an alarm on his watch, to gaze out the window to see if the front door of Ivan's home was sitting open. If he found it like that, he would have rushed out to locate his tormentor and steer him toward the hill, and the rocks below.

The front door stayed closed and Soulless was losing sleep of his own. Then he learned through an overheard conversation that Ivan's parents had installed a new lock on the door that could only be opened with a key, a key that Ivan didn't have access to.

Having suffered a setback, Soulless didn't quit, he came up with another plan. Several nights later a tragedy occurred when Ivan, his parents, three sisters, and his grandparents all were killed in a horrendous fire. It was ruled an act of arson and murder before the ashes were cool because paint thinner had been used to set the blaze. The combustible liquid had been poured all around the home and set afire to trap the family inside.

Soulless felt no remorse over having killed Ivan's family. His goal had been to kill Ivan, and he had accomplished it.

No one suspected him, nor could have imagined that a boy his age could have committed such a monstrous act. However, there was someone who knew what had happened. He was an older man who the adults steered clear of and who kept to himself.

One day as Soulless was walking home from school, the man appeared beside him and spoke.

"I saw you set fire to that house. Why did you do it?"

Soulless was torn between running away or lying. He did neither but spoke the truth and told the man about Ivan's persecution of him. To his surprise, the man smiled.

"You solved that problem," the man said, and walked away.

When a day passed and no one else confronted Soulless about the fire, he realized that the man was keeping his secret. He began visiting the man, who was an ex-KGB agent named Yuri. Soulless learned many valuable things from Yuri. He had become Soulless's mentor and had been the only friend he'd ever had.

Eventually, an investigation of the arson led to the arrest and conviction of a business partner of Ivan's father. The business partner had been stealing money from the company they owned together. The authorities claimed that Ivan's father must have become aware of the theft and threatened to see the man go to prison. The business partner admitted he was a thief but vehemently denied his guilt in setting the blaze. No one believed him and a jury sentenced him to a life of hard labor.

A year after Ivan's death, Soulless experienced a growth spurt that marked him as one of the taller boys in his age group. He was never picked on again, at least, not because of his size. Davies had picked on him. He now rested at the bottom of a dumpster. In a way he was fortunate. He died alone and his parents and siblings hadn't had to die with him.

Ivan's death had taught Soulless two valuable lessons. The first was that murder was a treasured tool that solved problems. Murder was also making him a rich man as he labored in his profession as an assassin. The second lesson was just as valuable—make things happen. Soulless had wasted weeks and lost sleep watching and waiting for something to happen, for Ivan to leave his home in a somnolent stupor. When he became proactive and burnt down the boy's house, his problem was over. This approach often necessitated the death of what others might refer to as innocents, but Soulless didn't see them as people, only as collateral damage.

He dreamt of Ivan sometimes. In the dreams he was bigger than Ivan, and instead of burning him to death, he beat him without mercy until he was bloody and unrecognizable. He awoke from those dreams while smiling.

REFRESHED FROM A FEW HOURS OF SLEEP, SOULLESS returned to searching for the tunnel that would take him to General Kwami's escape route.

Late in the afternoon he was in a shaft that seemed promising. Not only did it run on due course toward the region where the palace was located, but there were also rail tracks. The tracks were shiny in spots and looked newer than if they'd been installed back when the passageway was dug. Soulless's confidence in the route was shattered when the beam of his headlamp fell upon a pile of rock. At some point there had been a cave in along the tunnel.

He had already traveled over a mile only to be disappointed yet again. Worse than that was the possibility that he had indeed found the general's escape route. If he was in the right passageway that meant that his plan had no way to succeed. He'd have to go after the dictator above ground, where nearly a hundred men were guarding his target.

Soulless turned and hurried back along the way he'd just traveled. He had more than a full day's time left to search and there was no point wasting any of it. He would only admit failure when he had exhausted all of the possibilities.

He ate cold food from a can along with fruit, which was a pair of indigenous Kei apples. One of the yellow fruits was sweet and the other bitter. Soulless ate both of them completely. He'd once come close to starving and was loath to waste any food he had available.

After a short rest and a review of his notes, he continued his quest. Sunday morning came and found him too tired to continue. Soulless took another nap, ate another cold meal, then searched an area that he had already considered the least hopeful. Every one of the tunnels in the section faced away from the area where Kwami's palace was. Unless one of them curved around and made a 180 degree turn there was no way he would ever get close to his target.

Soulless was in the second of the passageways when the tunnel did just that. After walking on a progressively slanted surface that took him deeper underground, he came across light rail tracks. The tracks looked newer than the one's he'd seen before. They also curved in a long arc that had Soulless traveling toward the palace.

He fought the urge to be optimistic as the tunnel stretched on. Later, when his headlamp illuminated a handcar, he couldn't help but smile. Less than ten meters beyond the handcar was a steel door. He had done it. He had found the general's escape route. The door had six locks, was eight feet high and four feet wide. He could only speculate on how many inches thick it was, but he guessed that it could withstand any assault by a battering ram. Soulless didn't care how tough the door was. With the plan he had, it didn't matter. It only mattered that he was directly below the palace, which he was.

He shone his light past the door and saw that there was a cavern. He entered it and found more tunnels. Curious, he explored three of them and found that they also ran beneath the land where the palace was. One of them ended at a natural cave that had a small underground stream running through it. The additional tunnels would be put to good use.

HIS EYES HAD TO ADJUST TO THE SUN AS HE STEPPED from the mine. It was setting and looked large in what was a cloudless sky.

He made the long walk up the zig-zagging road and could hear that the old security guard was listening to the radio again. The man was unaware that he'd had a weekend visitor.

When Soulless took a better look at him through the binoculars he could see that it was a different old man than the one who had been there on Friday night. You'd think it would be difficult to find someone to sit in a booth for hours on end in the middle of nowhere. Instead, they likely lined up for the chance to do so in hope of getting a few dollars an hour. That amazed Soulless. He had always worked for himself and always made a good living doing so. Of course, his type of work was of a sort that few were willing, or able, to do.

The car was where he'd left it parked under a tree. The birds had used it for target practice, and he had to clean the windshield so he could see. He drove back to the city and took a room in a hotel. It was the same room Tanner had vacated earlier that morning. The room wasn't the only thing they had in common. They were both out to assassinate the same man. If Soulless's plan went the way he expected, he'd beat Tanner to the kill. He might also bring about Tanner's death, along with the death of many others.

Soulless wasn't going to shoot General Kwami. He was going to place a bomb beneath the palace. A bomb so powerful that it would cause the palace to collapse down into the mine. In fact, given how weak the underlying strata in the area was due to decades of mining, the whole thing might just open up into a bottomless pit and swallow the land, leaving a gaping black cavity of darkness in the quarry where the palace was erected. If that happened, anyone in the area would die along with the general.

Perhaps even a Tanner couldn't survive such a fate.

1 2
UP TO NO GOOD

Tanner showed up at the pickup spot to learn from one of the other men that they were going back to the compound a man short. He assumed that meant that Palmer had decided to return home until he saw him come walking around a corner.

Instead of Palmer, it was Younger who had decided that he'd had enough. That was too bad. Tanner would have liked it if Palmer had left and removed the possibility that he might have to hurt him.

The driver arrived with a new set of guards looking forward to their day off. Tanner managed to appear as concerned as the others when they were told about the attack on the border outpost. Everyone was relieved to learn that no one had been hurt.

Apparently, they had yet to discover that the rebels in Dubabi had suffered an attack on some of their troops. There would be consequences from that attack. Tanner hoped it resulted in the general's security being diverted so that he'd have an easier time of reaching Kwami.

He wasn't done causing trouble.

AFTER RETURNING TO THE COMPOUND HE WORKED A shift with Palmer and then pretended to bed down for the night.

In the early morning hours with everyone else asleep, Tanner slipped out of bed and got dressed. Over his khaki uniform he put on a black suit so that he could be mistaken for one of the palace guards. But not just any of the guards. He also donned a hat he had bought while in the city. It was the same type of wide-brim hat that their supervisor, Wes Walker, wore. He had also purchased the chewing tobacco Walker preferred. It would help to frame the man for what he was about to do. There were no cameras near the barracks other than one high up on a pole that kept watch over the area. The camera swiveled left and right and was easy to avoid by timing its arc.

Walker didn't merit a room inside the palace like Colonel Jaheem and the other soldiers, but he did have his own quarters near the barracks. It was a small structure that reminded Tanner of a log cabin, although it wasn't made of logs. It had one bedroom, a bathroom, and a tiny kitchen.

Tanner made his way over to it and stayed to the shadows until he was near the front door. He climbed over a side railing and onto the porch with great care, so as not to wake Walker. When he was at the front door, he strode forward and down the front steps. To anyone watching the monitor that carried the feed from the overhead camera, it would look as if Walker had left his home. Tanner was an inch shorter and weighed less than his supervisor but filmed from a distance at night he could pass for him, especially given the suit and the hat. The uniform he wore beneath the suit also gave him added bulk. He had put it on in case he ran into trouble and had to ditch the suit and blend in with the other guards.

A close call occurred as Tanner passed near the route taken by one of the wandering guard patrols. Tanner paused and took out the colorful package that contained the chewing tobacco. His head was down and his face hidden.

"Hello sir," said the guard. The man assumed that he was seeing Walker.

Tanner answered with a "Hmm," as he pretended to stuff a wad of tobacco in his mouth.

The guard suspected nothing and moved on. When he rounded the corner of a storage building that held supplies, Tanner followed. The building was his destination.

At the entrance, he reached into his pocket as if he were taking out a set of keys. Instead, he held nail clippers. The set of clippers had been modified to also contain a limited selection of lock picks. The lock on the storage building was a simple one that Tanner opened easily. He stepped inside and moved about with the judicious use of a penlight. He didn't need another patrolling guard to come along, see the beam of the flashlight, and find him inside.

Dry goods were stored in the building, foods such as rice, pasta, sugar, flour, and ground coffee. Tanner went about tampering with the coffee containers, while doing so in a subtle way. He wanted to make it look as if they had been fiddled with, but at the same time not make it too obvious. The natural conclusion would be that the coffee had been tainted, poisoned. Walker was a tea drinker, but most of the guards drank coffee, so did Colonel Jaheem.

He left the building and relocked the door behind him. Two minutes later he was walking up the steps of Walker's quarters. He slipped off the side of the porch as silently as he had climbed onto it earlier and moved back toward the barracks. He had to hide the suit and the hat. He chose to do so at the latrine.

The building that housed the latrine also held the showers. There was a set of twelve toilets. They were all in a row on one side of a wall without partitions between them. On the other side of the wall was a tiled area with several large drains and ten shower heads, five on each side. Again, there were no partitions, but the shower heads had been placed a meter and a half apart to allow room to move without bumping into the man beside you.

Tanner looked through a window and saw that the latrine was empty. It might not stay that way for long if any of his fellow guards rose in the middle of the night to urinate.

He timed his movements and entered the latrine without being captured by the camera, then rushed to the rear wall, which was made up of sections of teak wood. Tanner had noticed that one of the panels was loose. He intended to hide the suit and hat within the wall. He had another use for the items and needed to place them in a spot where he could later retrieve them.

He had the suit off and was about to pry the board loose when he heard a noise come from the area of the showers. Someone was back there.

Tanner bundled up the suit and set it on the side of a toilet. It wasn't completely hidden from view but wasn't out in plain sight either. He began walking toward the shower with his hand on his weapon.

"Who's over there?"

A familiar voice answered. It was Palmer. "Foxx? Is that you?"

Palmer appeared from around the corner with his right hand hidden behind him. He was still dressed in his underwear.

Tanner drew his weapon. "What's behind your back?"

Palmer held up his free hand. "Whoa, man, it's cool. Here, look." Palmer showed his right hand slowly. It was holding a satellite phone. "I couldn't stand being out of touch with my wife for another two weeks. You won't snitch on me, will you, bruv?"

Tanner relaxed and lowered the gun. Palmer was looking him over. "Why are you dressed so early?" He then looked behind Tanner as something caught his eye. "And what's that on the floor back there?"

Palmer walked over and saw the crumpled suit and the hat. He gave Tanner a puzzled look just as an alarm sounded off and lights blazed on outside.

"I'll keep your secret if you keep mine," Tanner said. Palmer answered with a nod before rushing over to the closet where the towels and soap were kept. He pried up a floorboard to reveal a hiding place for the satellite phone. Tanner brought the suit over and stuffed it inside the hole along with the hat. There was no time to do anything else. Something was going on and it could be an attack.

Palmer replaced the section of floorboard and they left the latrine. Since Tanner had his gun and was already dressed, he went to see what was going on while Palmer returned to the barracks to grab his clothes and gun. He gazed at Tanner with curiosity as they parted.

A guard was rushing past the barracks. It was the same man Tanner had encountered while dressed in the suit and pretending to be Walker.

Tanner shouted to him. "What's going on?"

The guard paused long enough to speak. There was excitement in his eyes. "They caught one of the rebels from Dubabi on our side of the border."

"Is he still alive?"

"Yeah," the guard said, and then he was gone.

Tanner smiled. Another part of his plan was bearing fruit. Walker was about to have a bad day.

13

BEYOND A SHADOW OF A DOUBT

SOULLESS MET WITH A REPRESENTATIVE OF THE PEOPLE he was working for on Sunday evening. He was surprised to see that his Arab contact was a white woman. She was good-looking without being flashy and had an Irish accent.

They met at a bar near the port that was doing a brisk business. Soulless and the woman looked like just another couple sharing a drink.

Despite the low light in the bar, Soulless wore sunglasses to hide his eyes. He hadn't shaved in over a week, and as a result, he had a decent beard coming in. There was also a cap sitting on his head. Between the shades, the beard, and the cap, he figured the woman would have trouble identifying him. That was fine. Since she was acting as a conduit between himself and his employers, he couldn't kill her to protect his anonymity.

He had spoken over the phone to his employer and given his request for explosives and timing devices. The woman had expertise in such matters and was there to gather more information. She didn't volunteer her name and Soulless didn't ask her for one. When he described how powerful the bomb needed to be, the woman shook her head.

"You need more than one package to achieve what you want. I'll recommend that you're given four packages. It would also be better if you placed them in different spots around the target area and staggered their detonation times."

"Why not one big bomb in one place?"

The woman winced at his use of the word bomb. Maybe she thought that calling them packages sounded better. Soulless didn't care. There was no one listening to their conversation so why not call them what they were?

"One package could work, or it could fail to do the job. By using more than one you also get more than one chance at getting the desired effect."

Soulless nodded his understanding. "Agreed. I'll also need two more bombs."

"That can be arranged," the woman said. Soulless noticed that she was staring at him. Maybe she was trying to figure out what he looked like without the beard and sunglasses.

"Can the last two explosives be similar to what they use in mining operations?"

"That would be ANFO—ammonium nitrate fuel oil. How powerful do the packages need to be?"

"I want to cause a cave-in."

"Then you'll need something more powerful. And may I ask why you need the two additional packages? Are they an added precaution against the target escaping?"

"Something like that."

"It seems unnecessary. The four original packages will obliterate anything around or above them."

"I still want them."

"I'll pass on your request."

"Can I get everything by Wednesday night?"

"That will be up to our employers. In any event, I'll meet back here with you at eight on Wednesday evening. Is there anything else?"

"Yes. The timers need to have long fuses."

The woman smiled. "They'll be electronic. You can set them to go off a minute later or a month later."

"Good. I guess we're done here."

"I'll see you on Wednesday," the woman said, and

stood. Before leaving, she held his gaze, then sent him a smile.

Soulless watched her go. She had a good body and he found himself wishing that they could spend some time together. He hadn't been with a woman since the ill-fated Heather in Arizona. He decided he would take some time off once the general was dead. He could use a period of rest under the Caribbean sun with nothing else to do but indulge his appetites.

That settled, his thoughts returned to the assassination of General Kwami. Four bombs instead of one. Yes, that should do the job. One of those bombs would be placed right outside the steel door of the general's escape tunnel. He'd have to consult the map he made while he was exploring the mine to find the best places to leave the other three devices. Four bombs. Yes. That would kill the general beyond the shadow of a doubt. The fifth and sixth bombs would serve their purpose as well.

Soulless left the bar and went back to his hotel room. He needed rest after barely sleeping during his search for the general's escape route. He also had another week of working in the mine ahead of him. He drifted off to sleep, confident that he would soon fulfill the contract.

THE REBEL CAPTURED NEAR THE BORDER WAS A bearded man with light skin. He'd surrendered without a fight once he realized he had three of the general's soldiers pointing weapons at him. His hands were bound at the wrists and he was on his knees.

Colonel Jaheem had brought him to the area they called the field. It was where the guards played soccer during their off-hours. The palace was on one side of the field and the barracks and other outbuildings were on the other side.

Everyone was up because of the blaring of the alarm. Tanner had taken off his shirt and left it behind in the showers, so that he wouldn't stand out from the others in his barracks who had been asleep. He was pleased to see that a few of them had taken the time to pull on their pants, but most were in their underwear, with eyes full of sleep.

They stood in a semicircle beneath floodlights as the colonel spoke to the prisoner. It was the first time Tanner saw the colonel out of uniform. He was wearing the slacks but was barefoot and shirtless. Although he wasn't a very big man, the colonel's muscles were defined, and his abdomen was chiseled.

"How many men were with you tonight?" the colonel asked in English. The same native language was spoken in Malika and Dubabi but with different dialects and accents. Most in the region also spoke English, so the colonel began his interrogation with that language.

Tanner expected the rebel to remain silent or curse at the colonel. Instead, the man answered in a calm voice. His English was good.

"I came alone."

"That's a lie."

"It's the truth. I was instructed to come alone by the note."

The man's mention of the note pleased Tanner. It looked as if the rebel was ready to talk without being coerced into it.

"What is this note you're talking about?" the colonel said.

"It was left in the pocket of a man who survived your attack yesterday."

The colonel raised an eyebrow. "We did not attack you. We were the ones who were attacked yesterday."

The rebel looked puzzled, then shook his head. "Five of our brothers were killed yesterday outside a restaurant. There was a note left behind telling us that someone here was willing to betray you if we helped them kill the general."

"And you were told that they would meet with you tonight?"

"Yes."

"Alone?"

"Our leader thought it might be a trap but sent me anyway. That's why I was alone... I guess my loss was acceptable to him."

"You're talking about Isaiah Danjuma, the rebel leader?"

"Yes."

"You must have had backup. At least one man."

The rebel shook his head as he lowered his eyes. Tanner thought he was lying. He would not have come alone because a mysterious note told him to do so. Curiosity might make you check it out, but it would be foolish to do so alone.

"No one here attacked you or left a note behind," the colonel said.

"Someone attacked us, and I saw the note."

"What's your name?"

"Keyon."

Walker moved up beside the colonel. There was a look of concern in his eyes as he stared at the rebel. He wore his suit slacks with a T-shirt and had on a pair of black slippers.

"Were you really attacked?" Walker asked the rebel.

"Yes. My friend was killed along with five others. Another man was injured but left alive. He was the one who had the note."

Walker spoke to the colonel. "Someone is trying to start a war between us and the Dubabi rebels."

"Maybe," the colonel said. He pointed at two men dressed in uniforms. Like himself, they were once child warriors for the general. One of them was older than the colonel and had graying temples. Tanner had heard him called Victor. Victor must have been almost in his teens when the general took him from his home to fight. The colonel addressed him. "Place this man in the pen until I decide what to do with him."

The "pen" was the closest thing the compound had to a jail. It was built after a guard went berserk and threatened others with a knife. It turned out the man was on drugs and had to be restrained. The colonel had a wire cage constructed. It had a wooden floor and ceiling and was ten feet square.

As the rebel, Keyon, was taken away, another of the colonel's soldiers ran up to him. When he saw Walker, he gestured for the colonel to move a short distance away before he began talking.

Whatever the new soldier said, it concerned Walker. The colonel turned his head to look at him while squinting in suspicion. Tanner saw that look and realized his plan to frame Walker was working. He wondered how Walker had come under suspicion so quickly. He didn't expect that to happen until after the coffee was found to have been tampered with. That could have taken days, until the kitchen's pantry needed replenishment. Then, he realized that the appearance of the rebel had caused the men manning the cameras to go over the recent video to see if any more rebels were about. Instead, they saw someone who appeared to be Walker going into the storehouse in the middle of the night.

The colonel looked around at the crowd that had gathered. "If you men aren't on duty go back to your barracks."

Tanner drifted away with the others. He wished he could view Walker's face when the colonel asked him about visiting the storehouse, but he had no valid reason to remain behind. As they neared the barracks, Palmer came up beside him and whispered.

"We need to talk."

"I know. Follow me."

There was a wooden shed past the barracks where the groundskeeper kept a riding mower and other such equipment. The area was beyond the view of the overhead camera and no one else was in listening range. Tanner leaned up against a wall of the shed and waited for the questions that were sure to come. He didn't need to wait long.

"Why did you have that suit, Foxx?"

Tanner had two choices. Neither of which was good. He could kill Palmer and hope that he wasn't connected to the man's murder. That was unlikely. They had been seen leaving the field together and had definitely been captured on camera walking toward the shed. His second choice was to admit the truth to Palmer. Palmer had already stated that he was eager to stop an assassin so he could claim a reward. The man needed money in a bad way and Tanner could be his ticket to get it.

He asked Palmer a question. "What do you think of me?"

"What do you mean?"

"If I told you that I would do something, would you trust me to do it?"

Palmer nodded. "I would. You don't strike me as being a bullshitter."

"Then listen to me. I will make sure that you get a million pounds if you help me. That's more than enough money to pay for your wife's medical care."

Palmer leaned back as he stared at him. "Where would you get that kind of money?"

"I was hired to kill General Kwami. I'll give you the money out of my fee."

Palmer continued to stare, then took a step back and raised his hands up slightly, as if to defend himself against an attack.

"If what you're saying is true, you're taking a hell of a chance admitting it to me. Even more so after what I said to you the other night at the bar."

"I'm taking a chance, yeah, but you said it yourself; I'm not a bullshitter. I'm here to kill the general and I'll do it any way I can."

"You're a professional assassin?"

Tanner nodded, while ready to pounce. If Palmer turned to flee, to shout out for help, he'd be forced to stop the man and kill him. He did not want to do that.

Palmer lowered his hands and relaxed. "You could have tried to kill me in the showers, instead you're trusting me. I'll trust you too. But how are you going to get to the general?"

"I need to get closer, to be assigned inside the palace."

Palmer gave him an incredulous look. "The palace? Foxx, you've only been here for weeks. I've heard it takes at least a year of proving yourself before anyone gets assigned there. And face it, you're not one of Walker's favorites."

"I know it's difficult to be assigned to guard the palace, but I've a plan in the works to do just that."

"And the suit was part of that plan?"

"Yeah. I framed Walker."

"Framed him? For what?"

"I made it look like he tampered with the food. They'll think he was trying to poison everyone."

"Shit. The colonel will kill him. How's that help you?"

"It helps *us*. We're in this together now."

"I guess that's true but answer the question. How does framing Walker get you closer to the general?"

Tanner smiled. "We're going to get on his good side."

14
THE LIFE YOU SAVE MAY BE
YOUR OWN

WALKER WASN'T SEEN MAKING HIS ROUNDS AND checking up on everyone as he usually did, and there was one of the colonel's fellow soldiers standing guard outside Walker's small home.

A rumor had started by the time the evening meal rolled around. The rumor was that Walker had been working with the rebel that had been captured and that he was going to help the rebels attack the palace. The first reaction by most of the guards was disbelief that their supervisor could be plotting against them. When it was stated that Walker had been seen outside by one of the guards just before the rebel was captured, doubt crept in about his innocence. Why would he be skulking around in the middle of the night?

Tanner monitored the gossip. When someone

167

mentioned that Walker might have been trying to poison them, he decided he had waited long enough to make his move. If he delayed any longer, the colonel or someone else might string Walker up on the flagpole, or just shoot him.

WALKER HAD SPENT THE DAY BEING INTERROGATED BY the colonel. The colonel had never liked Walker but had never thought he was capable of being disloyal. Walker had his position as head of the guards because he had aided the general during a time of crisis. If not for that and the general's affection for the man, the colonel would have been torturing Walker instead of simply talking to him.

His patience had worn thin when Walker had again denied being the man captured on video coming and going from the storehouse. He had lashed out by kicking Walker in the chest and sent him tumbling from the folding chair he was seated in. The older soldier, Victor, was there. His eyes widened when he saw that the colonel had lost his temper.

The colonel stood over Walker. The man was obviously lying. They had him on film leaving his quarters and going to the storehouse. A check of the inventory revealed that items had been tampered with and likely poisoned. Although unusual, Walker's visit to the storehouse wasn't remarkable and would have gone unreported. If the rebel hadn't been captured, most of the guards would have been poisoned in the coming days, and possibly the general as well.

Even if the general had avoided being poisoned, without the colonel and the other men to protect him, he would have been an easy target for assassination, especially if the assassin was someone he trusted.

Walker rose on all fours after being kicked. He looked up at the Colonel with a face red with rage.

"I didn't do what you're accusing me of! I would never hurt the general."

The colonel looked at him with disgust showing on his face. The general wouldn't want him to torture Walker, but he'd had a man beat the rebel named Keyon until he talked. Keyon admitted that he had not been alone and that he was working with a partner. He denied that Walker was that man and instead claimed it was another rebel who had fled after they realized they were outnumbered.

It was a lie. It had to be, and one way or another the colonel would get to the truth. He would love to be rid of Walker and take over his duties. He needed more than video evidence. He needed to make the man confess. He could have that if he tortured him.

With a confession from Walker even the general would want him dead.

The colonel's hand went to the handle of a knife sheathed on his belt. The time for talk was over. As he withdrew the blade, Victor reached over and gripped his wrist.

"Jaheem, think before you do something you can't take back."

The colonel shook free of Victor. "He's guilty, and I'm going to make him admit it."

Voices came from outside. Someone was speaking with the man at the door. The colonel looked through a window and saw two of the guards, Palmer and Foxx. Foxx was holding something in his hands that he had just removed from a plastic garbage bag. When the colonel realized what it was, he put his blade away and rushed toward the door while shouting an order to Victor.

"Keep an eye on Walker."

TANNER WATCHED COLONEL JAHEEM STEP OUT ONTO the porch and approach him. He held up the items he was holding. They were a crumpled black suit and a matching hat.

"Where did you get those?" the colonel asked.

"Palmer and I were kicking a soccer ball around when it rolled into the drainage ditch. I crawled down there to get the ball and found these clothes. Someone was trying to hide this."

The colonel just stared at the clothing. Finally, he reached out and took the hat. It looked like the type Walker wore. It had been meant to look like the type Walker wore.

Tanner lowered his voice. "Colonel, we've all heard the rumor about Walker being involved with the rebels. I don't believe it, and after finding these clothes lying around, I think something else has been going on." Tanner looked at the closed door of Walker's house. "I hope you didn't get carried away while… questioning him."

The colonel shook his head ever so slightly. He had come close to torturing a confession out of Walker. If he had done that to the general's pet thug and then found out that he was innocent—that would not have been good, not at all.

He took the suit from Tanner. "Who else knows that you've found this?"

"No one other than your man here," Palmer said. "We came right to you."

The colonel told Tanner and Palmer to say nothing about it and to go back to what they were doing. They left as the colonel returned inside the house.

～

THE COLONEL WALKED INTO THE HOUSE WITH THE suit and hat back inside the garbage bag. He laid them on the coffee table and walked into the kitchen. When he returned, he was holding a cold bottle of water and offering it to Walker.

Walker hesitated for only a moment before grabbing the bottle from his hand. He'd been denied food and water all day, and only allowed in the bathroom after the valve to the sink faucets had been cut off.

The colonel told Victor to leave the house so he could speak to Walker in private. The soldier obeyed and they were alone.

After draining the bottle, Walker looked up. "I swear I'm innocent, Jaheem."

"I believe you," the colonel said, and pointed at the coffee table.

"What is that?"

The colonel grabbed up the garbage bag and handed it to Walker. The supervisor of the guards made a face as he looked over the hat.

"This isn't mine. It looks new and the brim is different."

"What about the suit?"

"It's not one of mine either."

"Could it belong to one of your men?"

172

"I couldn't say. The men I have working in the palace all wear suits like this, but they're not all the same label."

"So that could belong to one of your men?"

Walker sighed. "I guess. Where did you find these items?"

"Those were just discovered in a drainage ditch by two of the guards, Palmer and Foxx. It looks like someone was trying to frame you."

Walker stared at the colonel before asking, "Was it you?"

The colonel straightened his back and looked indignant. "I would not do that. I know we've never gotten along, but I would never seek to cause you harm unjustly."

"Who did frame me?"

"I don't know yet. Something odd is going on. That rebel still insists that there was a note stating that someone inside the compound wants to form an alliance with the rebels. He also swears that they were attacked."

"And by impersonating me, they were trying to turn you against me. That has to be someone with inside knowledge about us."

"Yes."

"Why didn't they dispose of the suit in a way that it couldn't be found?"

"They probably thought that they had. It could

have stayed hidden in that drainage ditch for weeks. We were lucky it was found."

"I was *very* lucky. You were about to use your knife on me?"

"My job is to protect the general," the colonel said.

"That's my job too, Jaheem."

"There's one more thing," the colonel said, moving on, and he told Walker about the tainted supplies.

"POISON? ARE YOU SURE?" WALKER ASKED.

"Yes. That means we'll need new supplies and will have to have them guarded when we get them."

"It also means we have someone here who can't be trusted."

"Do you have anyone you suspect?"

Walker shook his head. "It could be anyone. There's a rumor that the rebels in Dubabi were being backed by Arabs who want to take over the region. If that's true, they could have offered one of our people a fortune to betray us. There might even be more than one traitor."

"Not my men. Your people," the colonel said. "My soldiers would die for the general."

Walker resisted rolling his eyes at that and held

up his empty water bottle. "I'm still thirsty, and this time I want a beer."

They moved into the kitchen. Walker grabbed two bottles of beer from the refrigerator and handed one to the colonel.

"We have to find whoever tried to frame me."

"And we can't rule out the men who guard the palace. That suit could belong to one of them."

"We can't trust anyone," Walker said. "Which is too bad, because we could use help figuring out who was behind this."

Both men took long pulls on their beers. The colonel lowered his bottle then used it to gesture at Walker.

"What you just said is wrong. There is someone we can trust."

"Who?"

"Palmer and Foxx. If either one of them was behind this, they wouldn't have come forward with those clothes."

"You're right," Walker said. "They also killed those six rebels. They can't be involved in this."

The colonel set his bottle on the table. "I have a suggestion."

PALMER SMILED AS HE LOOKED AT HIMSELF IN THE mirror. The black suit he had on fit him well. He and Tanner had been promoted to the status of palace guards. They were inside a clothing store in the city of Yousho. They would get three suits each and then be driven back to the compound by one of the ex-soldiers. The suits were off the rack but of good quality.

Palmer shook his head in wonder as he turned to Tanner. "You are one smart son of a bitch, Foxx. They reacted just like you said they would."

"It only makes sense to have us guarding the palace since they assume they can trust us."

"Where did you get the rat poison?"

"There was no poison. I only tampered with the packaging on the coffee to make it look as if it were tainted."

"No mate, the sugar was messed with too. They found that rat poison had been mixed in with it."

Tanner had been smoothing out a wrinkle in his suit jacket. He stopped in mid-movement at hearing Palmer's words. "Are you certain of that?"

"Yeah. There was poison."

An uncharacteristic expression of shock flashed across Tanner's features as he realized his deception was in fact a reality. Someone *had* poisoned the food. If he and the other guards had ingested the toxic cuisine, they'd be dead. Whoever had tainted the food would have done so for only one reason. They were after the general. There was another assassin inside the compound, or someone was out to grab power. Had he not come up with his plan to frame Walker, the unknown killer would not only have prevented him from fulfilling the contract on the general, but he might also have become one of the killer's victims.

"Palmer."

"Yeah?"

"I plan to make my move on the general the second he's in my sight. If I don't, I may never get the chance again."

"I'll back you up, but what if we're outnumbered by the soldiers?"

"Then they die," Tanner said. "They die."

15

THE LIE IS THE TRUTH

TWO UNIFORMED OFFICERS OF THE MALIKAN POLICE showed up at the mine on Monday morning. They were there to question Davies about an assault on a young woman in her apartment.

If the police were looking for Davies that meant that his body hadn't been discovered in the dumpster. Soulless assumed that it would never surface, and Davies would be labeled a violent thief and a fugitive.

His new supervisor was a quiet man named Richard. Richard had nothing against Soulless and didn't go out of his way to saddle him with unpleasant tasks. He recognized that Soulless was a good worker and paid him no undue attention. Had Davies had that attitude he would still be alive.

Soulless had been careful to leave no signs

behind that he had spent the weekend in the mine, or so he had thought. As he passed by the tank that held the diesel fuel for the air purification system, Soulless realized that someone might wonder why there was less fuel than there should be. If that happened, they might suspect it had been stolen and increase security on the weekends.

Puncturing the tank to claim the lower fuel level was a result of a leak might work, but the steel tank was tough, and it would be difficult to puncture it. An easier solution was to damage the gauge that measured the fuel level. Soulless accomplished that by using a rock and smashing the gauge.

The tank was situated near the entrance to the gravel road that the huge haul trucks used to travel to the area of the pit where they were loaded up. The gravel that comprised the road wasn't the normal pea gravel used in a home's driveway but were fist-sized chunks. Soulless used one of them to smash the gauge as a truck passed by. The gigantic vehicle blocked anyone's view of him. It was the size of a small house with tires that were twice the height of a man, while the truck's engine made enough noise to drown out his destruction of the gauge.

On his way into the mine he spoke to the man who was handing out equipment. He claimed to have seen a truck tire propel one of the gravel chunks against the gauge.

"How bad is the damage?" the man asked.

"The glass on the front of the gauge is cracked and the needle inside broke off. It's useless."

"I'll let the office know," the man said. "They'll have the fuel dealer replace it the next time he's around. You're lucky the rock didn't hit you."

"I ducked, the gauge didn't."

That settled the matter and avoided anyone becoming concerned about the missing fuel right away. Soulless only needed to make it through the week, collect the "packages" from the Irish woman, and use them to kill the general. He would have one more successful assassination under his belt and be that much closer to being considered the best assassin in the world, making everyone forget about the reign of Tanner. For just a moment, Soulless wondered where the assassin was. He would have been startled to learn that the legendary hit man was only miles away.

TANNER'S NEW DUTY INSIDE THE PALACE HAD PERKS other than the bump in pay and the wearing of better clothes. The work was easier, the food was of a higher quality, and the shifts were shorter. He and Palmer were given their own rooms so they could respond to trouble at any time of the night or day.

Along with the suits, they were given bulletproof vests, communication equipment, and rifles to supplement their handguns.

Although only one-story high the palace was enormous. Tanner and Palmer had been issued maps to study that detailed the structure's interior layout. They were expected to memorize it.

General Kwami's private five thousand square foot quarters were located at the center of it all. He had his own cook, maids, an indoor pool, and in prior years what amounted to a harem. The women were no longer there. At seventy-one, General Muhammad Kwami's carnal desires weren't as voracious as they once were. Since coming to work as a guard at the compound Tanner had heard that Kwami did have a woman brought in now and then, but it had become rarer and rarer. He'd also once been an avid horseman, which is why Colonel Jaheem was often seen riding a steed. Since the general had stopped riding, Jaheem took it upon himself to exercise the horses. There were two of them, both were large and beautiful animals.

If not for his control over the valuable platinum mine, Tanner guessed that Lawson and others interested in removing Kwami from power would have waited until the general died of natural causes. The man was clearly in decline. Then again, he could have gone on to live another twenty years. By hiring him to kill the general, Lawson had made certain that the general's days were numbered.

Someone else apparently had the same idea and had hired another assassin. Of course, there was always the possibility that the poisoning of the guards' food supply was an inside job. If so, it was likely someone close to the general who had designs on taking over leadership of the country once the dictator was dead.

Tanner's first guess was that Colonel Jaheem might have ambitions of the sort, but he rejected that idea almost immediately. Jaheem was a true believer, someone who had been indoctrinated to love and obey the general since he was a boy of eight. Lawson was right when he said that the general was like a father figure to the colonel. Besides, if the colonel wanted Kwami dead he could kill him easily.

It was the colonel who took the general his meals and he spent hours with the man every day. No one else was allowed to be near the general unless Colonel Jaheem was present along with another of the ex-child soldiers. It was one of the things that would make killing the general a challenge.

Since beginning his stint as a palace guard, Tanner learned that no one was allowed in the presence of the dictator if they were armed. This did not include the supervisor of the guards, Walker. It also did not include the colonel and his men. It *would* include a new man like Tanner. Tanner would have to find a way around that. He surely didn't need a gun to be able to kill someone. However, having a firearm would be helpful if he hoped to survive and escape after killing his target.

When he was finally allowed to meet the general, he would be searched for other weapons as well, such as knives or a wire he could use as a garrote. They could deny him the tools of his trade, but he possessed the knowledge, skill, and experience to kill without any weapons.

Palmer had been true to his word and had not betrayed him. Tanner would do his best to see that the man survived and would pay him the million pounds as promised. Palmer's help could be vital when the time came to fulfill the contract.

Tanner had risked using Palmer's satellite phone to make contact with Lawson and inform him of Palmer's involvement and the deal he had made. Lawson had been pleased to learn that Tanner had wrangled himself into the palace and within striking distance of the general. Lawson said that he would cover the payment to Palmer's family and that Palmer would be included in the extraction plans when it was time for Tanner to be picked up and taken out of the country. He also had news that made getting to Kwami an urgent matter.

"Soulless? Are you sure?"

"That's what we've heard from a spy we have in a foreign government. The assassin named Soulless has been hired to kill General Kwami. He could be doing as you are and pretending to be one of the guards. All we know is that he's white, but we have no photos or a description of the man, so watch your back, Tanner."

Poisoning an entire group of people to get to one man seemed like something Soulless would do. Tanner realized that causing mindless mayhem and a disregard for innocents was standard operating procedure for Soulless. It was a brutal if effective way to go about fulfilling a contract and one he would never employ.

He didn't think that Soulless was a guard. There were only three other white men in the compound who were new guards and two of them knew each other and were friends. The third one had been Younger, but Younger had quit and left the country. No, Soulless must be working on a different plan to kill the general. Given the man's reputation for causing chaos, Tanner knew that anything might happen. The one thing that wouldn't occur would be for Soulless to kill the general before he could. He was a Tanner. A Tanner never failed.

Tanner's duties inside the palace involved patrolling the hallways or walking around the perimeter and grounds of the sprawling home. Covering the distance on foot took nearly half an hour and involved walking over a mile. Living down in the pit was like being at the bottom of a gigantic stone cereal bowl. The sides of the pit were over a hundred feet high and the wall built on top of them added another sixteen feet.

There were guard shacks on each side of the palace as well as a central security office inside. A bank of screens was monitored by the ex-soldiers and they displayed the feeds from over forty cameras. Despite the high security there were no cameras inside the general's private quarters. After becoming aware of that fact, Tanner decided that it would be the perfect place to kill the man. The trick would be getting in and out alive.

Colonel Jaheem and Walker had talked to Tanner and Palmer in private when they were picked to become palace guards. Along with their normal duties, they were to keep an eye out for anyone acting unusual.

"You're looking for the person who poisoned the food?" Palmer asked.

"That's right," Walker said. "That same bastard tried to frame me and must be out to kill the general."

"We have to identify them," the colonel said.

Tanner and Palmer were having breakfast in the small mess hall inside the palace when Walker approached them with Colonel Jaheem.

"You'll be reporting to the colonel this afternoon," Walker told them. "I'll be going into the city with several men to buy new rations to replace the food we had to throw out."

The colonel told Walker that he would send two of the soldiers along as well. "In case the rebels are about and looking to cause more trouble."

"Assign Victor to me; he's a good man," Walker said.

"I'll do that," the colonel agreed.

Tanner was glad to hear that Walker would be away for a time with several guards. If an opportunity arose to kill the general, there would be a few less men to have to deal with.

After reaching the city, Walker handed a list of what was needed to one of the soldiers who would be helped by three of the regular guards. A second soldier, Victor, stayed with the vehicles they were using. One was a Hummer with right-hand steering, along with a van to ferry all the supplies.

Walker left the Hummer and headed on foot to a shop several blocks from the supermarket that carried the brand of chewing tobacco he favored. After buying the tobacco, he left the shop and looked around carefully. When he was certain no one was paying any undue attention to him, he crossed the street and walked into an alleyway.

There was a recess halfway down the alley where space had been left to make room for a dumpster. A man was standing there. He had dark skin, deep-set brown eyes, a receding hairline, and was dressed in jeans and a hoodie. The hood was up to keep his face in shadows. His name was Isaiah Danjuma. He was the leader of the rebels who currently controlled the tiny nation of Dubabi. He and Walker had been friends when they were both young mercenaries. Walker had recently renewed the friendship when he realized that Danjuma could be a useful ally in his ambition to take over leadership of Malika.

Tanner had framed Walker for poisoning the food, little realizing that the man was actually guilty of doing it. It was Walker who had laced the sugar with rat poison. Thanks to Tanner, not only was the man thought to be innocent, but he'd been given the responsibility of gathering food to replace that which he had poisoned. At the same time, Walker had assigned Tanner to work inside the palace, Tanner, a man who could ruin his plans and make certain that he never became leader of Malika. Their separate machinations had unintentionally aided each other.

Walker greeted Danjuma with a broad smile. Danjuma returned the greeting, but there was worry in his eyes.

"Until I received word from you, Walker, I was afraid that the general had discovered your intentions."

"Kwami is an old man who has lost his fire. He won't know a thing until I take his life."

"Why did you not stop the attack on us last week?"

"We did not attack you. I don't know what that was about. I also never asked to meet with you at the compound as your man, Keyon, claimed."

"Is Keyon dead?"

"Yes. Colonel Jaheem tortured him then killed him."

"It is no great loss, but I need to know who attacked us."

"There's an unknown person or persons out to cause trouble. It might even be the general's son."

"The prince? Why would he send men to kill my people?"

"Maybe he was trying to start a war with Dubabi

so he could take it over and regain territory his father lost. There are those in the west who would give him aid and possibly troops. In return, he could give them platinum from the mine and replace the general as ruler."

Danjuma looked skeptical. "He would kill his own father?"

"Maybe he's tired of running the country without getting the credit. If so, he's waited too long to make his move. I plan to strike soon and kill the general."

"How soon?"

"Tomorrow. I'll have everything in place. Are you ready to do your part?"

"Of course. There's just the matter of timing to discuss."

"The general will meet with Colonel Faheem and myself tomorrow as we introduce him to a pair of new palace guards. I'll use that opportunity to kill him."

"What about the colonel?"

"He'll be handled, as will the new guards. I may spare them though; they are useful men."

"What time is the meeting?"

"At two p.m."

"I'll attack three minutes later. There's still the problem of the army. They will come to the general's aid once they learn that the palace is under attack."

"They won't. I'll make certain of it before going

to the meeting."

"How?"

"I have someone I can trust. He will take care of the guards in the security office moments before the meeting. They won't have time to send out an alarm."

"And the prince?"

"The general's son is a great one for the arts and high-tech and seeks to be loved by the people, but he's not a fighter. He'll flee the country once he knows I'm in charge. Eventually, he'll be hunted down and killed."

Danjuma grinned. "We'll own this region after tomorrow. Once you're in control, I'll send you people to labor in the platinum mine for free."

"And we'll use the profits to buy arms that will strengthen us. But before any of that can happen, I have to kill my employer."

Danjuma gripped his friend's arm and stared into his eyes. "Do not fail."

Walker met his gaze. "The general will die."

THE MEETING ENDED AND DANJUMA TURNED AND walked off down the alley. Walker went out the way he had come, turned left, and nearly collided into the ex-child soldier, Victor.

Walker was surprised, then looked annoyed. "Why are you here? You were to stay with the vehicles."

"They have the official seal on them. No one would dare touch them. I thought you might need help if Danjuma tried to betray you."

"He has no reason to do that."

"And will he attack tomorrow?"

"Yes."

Victor looked pleased. "Tomorrow will be a grand day."

"If we all do our part, yes."

Victor closed his eyes and sighed. "I've waited so long for revenge."

General Kwami and Colonel Jaheem believed Victor to be unquestionably loyal to the general. However, Victor had always harbored hatred for the dictator. Unlike Jaheem and the other child soldiers who were ripped away from families steeped in poverty and abuse when they were eight or younger, Victor had been twelve. He'd come from a loving home where he was cared for, and despite the brainwashing and lies he'd been fed by the general, he still remembered his childhood well.

After the war, Victor discovered that his home had been destroyed and his family was dead. He stayed with the general out of necessity as the country had been in chaos and he was still just a boy.

192

With the general he had food and a roof over his head. Although hatred for the man churned in his breast, Victor kept his feelings to himself and stayed with his fellow soldiers. When thoughts of gaining revenge against the general surfaced, he would stuff them back down. He'd had numerous opportunities to kill the man over the years, but none in which his own death wouldn't have soon followed.

Months earlier, while in the presence of the general, Victor let his guard down and his face had revealed the detestation he'd felt for the man. Walker had noticed.

Walker had approached Victor inside a bar while both men were enjoying time away from their duties. He asked Victor a question that shocked him.

"You hate the general, don't you?"

Victor had looked around expecting to see the colonel lurking nearby. There was no one other than the other bar patrons.

"He stole me away from my family and placed me on a battlefield. There were hundreds of us then, all boys no older than thirteen. He threw us at the enemy like so much cannon fodder, like we were less than nothing. Only seventeen of us remain; the rest either died in battle or later from their wounds. I was a happy child before that, Walker, and I've never been happy since."

Walker had leaned in and spoke in a whisper.

"I'm going to kill the general and take his place as leader of the country. Will you help me?"

Victor answered without hesitation. "Yes. I want to see him die."

WALKER AND VICTOR RETURNED TO THE HUMMER. Shortly after, the other men appeared with the new supplies and they were on their way back to the palace. As he drove through the streets of Yousho, Walker imagined himself returning to the city as the country's ruler.

In time, he would also betray Danjuma and take over Dubabi as well. He was forty-four and in good health. Adolf Hitler had become the Chancellor of Germany at the same age. Ten years later he was on the verge of world domination. Walker's ambitions were just as grand. He sat back in his seat and imagined himself older and reigning over all of Africa, then Europe, and eventually, the world. It was a recurring fantasy, and he was one day away from taking the first step to make it a reality. General Mohamed Kwami, leader of Malika, would die at his hand, and the reign of Wes Walker would begin.

PACKAGES DELIVERED

SOULLESS HAD DRIVEN TO THE MINE ON HIS motorcycle instead of crowding in with the other workers on the transfer truck. This allowed him to come and go as he pleased during the week, although he still slept in the dormitory-style quarters provided to the workers.

As they had agreed to at their first get-together, Soulless returned to the bar on Wednesday evening to meet with the Irish woman who would supply him with the explosives he needed.

His beard had grown in fuller and he again wore a cap with sunglasses. The woman was seated at a table near the back and away from others. The blouse she had on displayed a hint of cleavage and she was wearing a skirt instead of slacks. She also wore more makeup than she had on their first meeting. On the seat beside her was a black backpack.

They greeted each other with nods. Before they could speak, a waiter came over to find out what Soulless wanted to drink. He ordered a Guinness and the man went to get it for him.

"Do you have the bombs?"

The woman winced again at his use of the word, but nodded yes, as her eyes shifted to the backpack.

"Everything is in there. I'll need to instruct you on how to set the timers."

Soulless's drink arrived. He ignored it as he stared at the backpack. Whatever was in it filled it completely and had an oblong shape. "I'm surprised that you were able to fit everything inside that rucksack."

"The packages are compact but extremely powerful. They will do what you want them to do. In fact, I'd say that they are more than you need."

"Overkill is fine. Failure isn't."

They left the bar and walked a short distance to where a van was parked. Soulless carried the backpack. It was heavier than it looked. As the woman climbed into the van through a side door, he couldn't help but admire the view of her from the rear. She was desirable and he was tempted to try to make their relationship more than business. He had also noticed her studying him in a manner that was other than professional. But no, if that happened, she would be able to identify him, beard or no beard.

The van's rear windows were blacked-out and the door locked securely. There were two metal folding chairs and a card table. The Irish woman took a seat and opened the backpack to reach inside to pull out a gray case. When she opened the case after setting it on the table, Soulless saw several objects seated in foam cutouts. The six bombs he had ordered were cylindrical and about the size of softballs. The other objects resembled pocket watches.

"They don't look like much," Soulless noted.

The woman smiled. "They could level several city blocks. You'll have no problem collapsing a labyrinth of mine shafts."

She spent the next few minutes teaching Soulless how to handle the timers and finished by issuing a warning.

"Set the timers so that you'll have plenty of time to be out of the area… I wouldn't want to see you get hurt."

Soulless stared at her from behind the dark lenses he wore. "What's your name?"

She smiled again, and there was warmth in it this time. "You can call me Gwen."

"And did our employer give you my name?"

"I was told that you go by the name Soulless."

"I don't, but I was given that name by someone and it has followed me around. I don't mind it, and one phony name is as good as another."

Gwen repacked the bombs. Afterward, she grabbed a pen and a pad of paper that was on the table and began writing out an email address, along with the password needed to access it as an owner. She handed that to Soulless.

"I do solo work as well. If you need something exotic, like these packages, leave a message in the draft folder and I'll reply within a day."

"I don't expect to be in Africa much longer."

"Neither do I. Next week I'll be in Rio, after that, I might fly to the United States. It pays to stay on the move in my business."

"It's the same for me," Soulless said.

They stared at each other for a moment, but Soulless had already made up his mind, and nothing would happen.

Gwen unlocked the van and Soulless stepped out. As he was walking away, Gwen said, "Good luck."

He raised up a hand in acknowledgement but kept walking. Now that he had the tools he needed to do so, his thoughts had turned to causing the death of General Kwami.

Tanner and Palmer were informed that they would be given the honor of meeting General Kwami the next day. Walker told them to make certain that their suits weren't wrinkled and to shine their shoes. It was the chance Tanner had been waiting for. The news pleased him but made Palmer nervous.

"What if he has too many men around him?"

"We'll be outnumbered. I expect that. It won't matter."

"Why won't it matter?"

"They won't expect us to try anything. If they did, they would never let us near him. We'll have the element of surprise."

"That might help if we were going to be armed, but we won't be, and the soldiers will have guns."

"I don't need a gun to kill. I'm also very good at it."

"How many... what do you call them... Contracts? How many have you had?"

"Palmer, I've been doing this for most of my life, and there's no one better at it. If there are ten soldiers guarding the general, I'll still kill him. I don't fail."

Palmer sighed. "You'll have me helping you. I just hope I come out of this alive."

"That's the plan."

"Plan? What plan? It looks like you're playing it by ear to me."

"There's an old saying—no plan survives contact with the enemy. Plans can only take you so far, action, experience, and daring can defeat superior odds."

"And you've never failed?"

"Never. No enemy survives contact with me."

Palmer laughed. "You're a cocky bloke, Foxx."

"So I've been told."

17
ALL SYSTEMS ARE GO

THE NEXT DAY, THE REBEL LEADER, ISAIAH DANJUMA, assembled over two hundred of his rebels near the border. Along with guns and rifles they had an old Soviet Katyusha rocket launcher that had been built in 1978. Danjuma had acquired the vintage weapon from an arms dealer he'd contacted over the internet. It was bolted on to the rear of a tow truck and he only had two rockets for it. The rockets were heavy, over four feet in length. They looked as old as the launcher.

They would destroy the main gate to allow access down into the pit. They would also put terror into the guards.

At the same time, more of Danjuma's rebels were keeping the nearest army base busy. They had set a fire near the base as a distraction while also damaging the cellphone and radio towers.

Danjuma hadn't been comfortable relying on Walker to disrupt the palace's communication system. If the army base became aware that the palace was under attack too soon it would be disastrous. The added soldiers would overwhelm the rebels by giving them an enemy at their backs.

Danjuma's satellite phone rang. It was the man he'd left in charge at the army base. They had started the fire and taken out the communication towers.

"There's a chance they might send someone to the palace to check on things once they lose contact."

Danjuma hadn't considered that. But it was easy enough to deal with.

"Before leaving the area, fell trees to block the roads leading from the army base. That will slow them down. Better yet, keep watch on the road that leads here. If you see any army vehicles headed this way in the next hour, attack them and slow them down. That should buy us the time we need."

The man acknowledged the order and the conversation ended. Danjuma checked his watch. It was 1:51. They would attack in twelve minutes.

Tanner and Palmer had been given the evening watch. That was so they would be free in the afternoon to meet the general. General Kwami had been told of the attempt to poison his guards and of the framing of his trusted protector, Walker. He wanted to meet the two men who had cleared Walker's name.

The truth was that the general should have been introduced to them sooner. Colonel Jaheem wisely arranged for the general to know the face of every man who worked in the palace. That way, if someone approached the general who was unfamiliar to him, he would know that they didn't belong. The introductions had been delayed because Jaheem had been distracted by trying to ferret out who attempted to frame Walker.

Colonel Jaheem was loyal to the general and loved the man like a father. He would be horrified if he knew he was entering the general's private quarters with men who wanted to take the general's life. Colonel Jaheem was with Victor, Walker, Palmer, and Tanner. All four men intended to see the general dead before they left the palace.

Tanner followed Colonel Jaheem into a windowless book-lined room that was fourteen feet high with bookcases that stretched from floor-to-ceiling. There were thousands of books, all were bound in leather and made for an impressive sight. An elaborate chair was set against one wall and was set on a six-foot circle of polished marble. The chair was carved from what looked like a solid piece of wood and was the size of a throne. It had a cushion on its seat and was surrounded by the bookshelves on either side. More books were above it.

Along with the chair was a pair of leather sofas. Each sofa was long enough to seat six comfortably. They were in the middle of the room on a Persian carpet and were flanked on both sides by end tables. The marble surfaces of the tables matched the marble beneath the wooden chair. Hanging from the ceiling was an enormous crystal chandelier. The finial at its bottom gleamed and was made of gold.

The room was the first sign of luxury that Tanner had seen inside the palace. The outside of the sprawling structure was made of brick and the interior walls were just as bland. It appeared the general only gave thought to making things aesthetically pleasing when it concerned his private quarters.

After a cursory pat down to make certain they weren't carrying weapons, Jaheem told Tanner and Palmer to wait in the room along with Victor and Walker. He would have the general with him when he returned. He had already schooled them on the proper way to greet and address the general. After saying hello, they were not to talk unless the general asked them a question. The colonel took his exit by walking through a door on the other side of the room, which was forty feet away.

As he waited, Tanner drifted about the room. He was looking for something he might use as a weapon. He would have this one chance to kill Kwami, and although unarmed he was as lethal a man that had ever drawn a breath.

An examination of the books revealed something interesting; they had never been read. Their spines were crisp and some even smelled new. The general wasn't a reader, he just wanted to give off the impression that he was.

There was nothing in the room that might be used as a good makeshift weapon. However, the Colonel had a sidearm, as did Walker and Victor. Tanner decided that Victor might be his best bet. The man appeared nervous and kept licking his lips. Maybe he was intimidated by the general.

Walker gestured for Victor to join him in a corner of the room and they began talking privately. Tanner took that opportunity to whisper to Palmer.

"Grab a weapon the first opportunity you get, then shoot anyone I haven't already killed. And remember, they have on vests like we do."

"The other guards will be on us like white on rice once they hear the shots."

Tanner shook his head. "Not only are there no cameras here, but the rooms in this suite are soundproof."

"Are you sure?"

"I took a look at the doorframe and the walls as we entered. They're extra thick, likely with soundproofing."

Palmer looked around. "All of these books will also act to absorb the sound too."

"Yeah," Tanner said.

Colonel Jaheem returned. The general was with him. At Seventy-one, General Mohamed Kwami was a shadow of his former self. The dictator had been a barrel-chested giant of a man in his prime. The old man entering the room beside Jaheem was shrunken, wrinkled, and stooped over, while supporting himself on a cane.

Jaheem followed the general over to the carved chair, where the old man took a seat on his throne. Despite the loss of vitality the last few years had taken on the man, General Kwami's eyes were alert.

Colonel Jaheem gestured for everyone to approach. Palmer sent Tanner a nervous glance as they moved closer. Tanner ignored him, as he was watching Victor from the side of his eye. The strap on Victor's holster was already undone. It would be a simple matter to take the man's gun. Tanner and Palmer stood before the general as Jaheem began introducing them. After shifting his weight slightly, Tanner's right hand moved in a blur toward Victor's weapon.

VICTOR FELT MORE ANXIETY THAN HE HAD SINCE being a boy in a war zone. The time had finally arrived when he would see the general dead. As much as he'd love to kill him, that pleasure would go to Walker. Victor had been given the task of killing Colonel Jaheem. It would sadden Victor to do so. He and Jaheem had once been true friends, and he respected him as a soldier. He'd once seen Jaheem in a firefight with three adult men and he had come out on top. Jaheem had been only eight at the time and was fearless. Victor intended to make his death a quick one by shooting him in the head. It was the only way really, since the colonel was wearing a bulletproof vest.

He looked to his left. Past the guard named Palmer stood Walker. Walker was looking back at him, and Victor could see that his hand was easing toward his weapon. Walker gave a slight nod, then mouthed the word, "Go!"

Victor drew his weapon, and all hell broke loose.

18

SIC SEMPER TYRANNIS

SOULLESS HAD REENTERED THE MINE THAT MORNING only to disappear down an unused tunnel. Hidden within the folds of the oversized coveralls he wore were five of the cylindrical bombs the Irish woman, Gwen, had given him. The day had come to kill the general and fulfill the contract.

The beard was gone. He had shaved that morning and was looking forward to never having to work in the mine again. Manual labor was not something he enjoyed. He waited a day after receiving the bombs before using them. Friday was payday at the mine. No one would call out sick. He wanted every person who knew his face to be present.

He placed the first bomb at a point where he believed the eastern rim of the old copper mine was located. He estimated that it was roughly where the main gate guarded the entrance. Destroying that first would make sure that the general couldn't be driven away from the palace. Bomb two was placed near the western rim, and bomb three was inside the general's escape tunnel beneath the center of the pit. If the first two blasts didn't kill or injure the general, he would flee to his escape route only to meet death as the third bomb exploded. The fourth bomb was secured in a passageway that was beneath the northern rim of the compound. If there was anything left to destroy, the fourth detonation would obliterate it. The distances between the bombs was great and required Soulless to navigate through numerous passageways. The work took hours.

As for the fifth bomb, that was left at a key spot within the platinum mine. It would destroy the ventilation system and cause a cave-in. His fellow workers knew his face well; they could not be allowed to live.

Soulless had set the timers on the first two bombs so that they would detonate one minute apart. He then allowed Kwami eight minutes to make it into his escape tunnel. If for whatever reason the dictator stayed in the palace to hunker down, the fourth bomb would make that a moot point. Anyone within the walls of that structure would surely die.

Before leaving the mine, Soulless stripped off his

coveralls. As he was stepping on the elevator to head up to the surface, the new supervisor, Richard, ran up to him.

"Brockton! Where the hell have you been all day?"

Soulless waited until the man was close enough, then he freed a knife he had on his belt, grabbed Richard by the throat, and slid the blade between Richard's ribs several times in quick succession. Richard groaned and fell to his knees, then was sent sprawling onto his back by a kick to the chest from Soulless. The man was still alive and could tell someone who it was that had stabbed him. It didn't matter. The same bombs that would destroy the palace could cause cave-ins within the mine. If not, Soulless had something else in mind to do the trick. Anyone underground would die.

After reaching the surface, Soulless disabled the mine elevator, along with the smaller lift used for inspections. He then came upon two men. One was an engineer and the other a welder. They were standing while leaning over a folding table with their heads together as they puzzled over something on a laptop computer. They were so engrossed in what they were discussing that they never noticed Soulless until he placed a bullet in the back of one of their heads. The second man was frozen in shock and died two seconds later.

The sound of the shots was heard inside the office trailer. The mine manager and another supervisor stepped out onto the small platform above the metal steps and looked around. Soulless walked toward them with the gun concealed. He knew that the bodies of the men he had just killed were hidden from the view of the men at the trailer. He also knew he needed to get closer to them before he could use the gun again.

The mine manager called to him. He was an older black man who was going bald. "Did you hear two loud bangs?"

Soulless cupped his ear, pretending that he couldn't hear him. It seemed reasonable. Over on the other side of the pit the waste rock was being bulldozed into piles that would later be loaded onto the haul trucks. The work made a lot of noise. As the mine manager repeated his question, Soulless drew within fifty feet of them.

"I said, did you hear two loud bangs?"

"Yeah."

"What was that?" the supervisor asked.

Soulless took out his weapon as he drew closer. "Those bangs were the sound made by this gun." He caught the supervisor with two shots to the chest. The mine manager had turned to flee back into the office. Soulless hit him with a pair of bullets between the shoulder blades and he tumbled down the stairs to lie on the ground moaning. A final shot to the head finished him.

Inside the trailer was the mine manager's female assistant. She was an older white woman with an Australian accent. She was in a state of panic. Her eyes were wet with tears, and she was taking quick little breaths, as her hand frantically searched for something inside her purse. A look of relief came over her as she found what she'd been searching for. When her hand came out of the purse, Soulless saw that she was holding a container of pepper spray. She squeezed the trigger and a jet of the disabling fluid shot forth. She had aimed directly at Soulless's face. The stream traveled a fair distance but lacked the energy to hit its target. The arc of the pepper spray petered out and the fluid dribbled onto the floor at Soulless's feet. He raised up the gun and placed a bullet between the woman's wet eyes.

The office phone rang a dozen times before stopping. That was followed by the sound of an engine approaching slowly as it made its way down the zig-zagging road. It was coming from the guard shack. On the weekends tired old men stood guard. That was not the case when the mine was open and operating. There would be two men on duty. They would be young, physically intimidating, and armed.

Soulless left the trailer and looked up and to his right. He could see the guards weaving their way down to investigate the sound of the gunshots. While reloading, he strolled out to the narrow, paved path that connected with the road.

When the guards were nearing the bottom of the road, Soulless stood in the center of the path with his weapon raised in a Weaver stance. He was waiting for the vehicle to come into view around a curve.

It was a golf cart with a Plexiglas windshield. The eyes on the two men riding in it expressed the surprise they were feeling as they came around the curve and spotted Soulless. He opened fire as the guard who was driving hit the brakes. Bullets passed through the flimsy windscreen and struck both guards. The driver suffered three wounds to his upper torso as another round chewed apart his left ear. The passenger was struck in his right arm as he drew his weapon. After that, he lost his grip on the gun and it slipped from his hand. He abandoned the golf cart and hit the ground beside it. Before he could scramble away, Soulless shot him again, hitting him in the side.

Moments later, everyone near the mine was either dead or trapped below ground because they couldn't access the elevators. Soulless needed everyone dead because they knew what he looked like. The men trapped below ground would have to die as well. And while the structural damage caused by the four bombs might cause a cave-in and kill them all, Soulless couldn't chance there being survivors. That was what the fifth, and the sixth and final bomb were for.

Along with the men in the mine, there were the truck drivers who transported the mined ore and also the waste rock. They ran on a schedule that would see them returning to the mine within the next half hour for another pickup. They would die as well, but not with the use of bullets.

Soulless straddled his motorcycle. He was headed up the footpath that led to the lake. Before taking off he checked his watch. The first bomb would be going off soon, ensuring the death of General Kwami, along with anyone else unfortunate enough to be near him.

TANNER HAD BEEN REACHING OUT TO GRAB VICTOR'S weapon when the soldier surprised him and drew it himself. The next shock came when Victor aimed the gun at Colonel Jaheem. While that was happening, Walker had taken out his own weapon intending to shoot the general. Tanner saw Walker's intention. He gripped Victor's wrist and redirected his aim just as he fired. His round struck Walker in the arm that was holding the gun. Walker's round missed and took a chunk out of the carved wooden chair the general sat in. Had the round been two inches lower, the general would have died. It was not for the likes of Walker to kill the dictator; that was Tanner's job. He had taken the contract, and as a Tanner, he'd rather die than fail.

COLONEL JAHEEM WORE A LOOK OF ASTONISHMENT AS he drew his weapon. Two men he trusted fully had just attempted to kill him and his beloved general.

He pointed his weapon at Victor. The older soldier was being disarmed by Tanner. At the same time, Palmer was picking up the weapon dropped by Walker. Jaheem fired twice; one bullet struck Victor high in the chest just above his vest while the other tore open his throat. He collapsed at the feet of the general. Jaheem, believing that Tanner and Palmer were on his side never noticed Palmer taking aim at him. He died from a shot to the head that killed him instantly.

A TOTAL OF SEVEN SECONDS HAD PASSED SINCE Victor had drawn his weapon. Victor lay dying, Colonel Jaheem was dead, and Walker was bleeding out from a wound to his throat. He had fallen back against the lower shelves of a bookcase with his hands gripped to his throat as he tried to stem the tide of blood rushing from his wound.

I'm dying, Walker thought, and the idea seemed absurd to him. He couldn't die. He was going to be ruler of Malika, all of Africa, ruler of the world! A sensation of coldness enveloped him as his vision faded. As the darkness swallowed him, his eyes shed tears of self-pity.

TANNER WATCHED WALKER DIE AS PALMER KICKED Colonel Jaheem's gun away. There was no doubt that Jaheem was dead, but training dictated that you not leave a loaded weapon near an enemy.

While the gunplay had been happening, General Kwami had reached his left hand over the side of his ornate chair and pressed a button that looked like a part of the chair's design. It was a switch that would cause the chair to swivel around on its marble platform. It was intended as a way for the general to escape the room if trouble broke out. It had not been designed to work if a body were lying on the platform.

The chair spun counterclockwise only to come to a stop as it hit the chest of the prone and dying

Victor. The motor powering the chair was formidable. It created steady pressure on Victor and there was a loud cracking sound as his spine broke. The chair gained an inch as Victor died, but his bulk was still in place and preventing it from going any farther.

The general released a string of curses in his native language. He had a gravelly voice. Having realized that the chair would not spin him out of harm's way, he looked up at Tanner, then Palmer.

"I will give you anything you want if you let me live."

Tanner answered him by pressing the barrel of Victor's gun against his head and pulling the trigger. General Mohamed Kwami, longtime leader of Malika was dead. The contract was fulfilled.

19

IGNORANCE IS BLISS

Isaiah Danjuma was unaware that Walker was dead. Had he known, it would not have changed his decision to attack the palace. After all, he was planning to kill Walker and take over control of Malika. Walker had just been a useful tool to gain intelligence about the palace's defenses.

Walker had not been the only one who harbored dreams of becoming a great leader and a powerful man. And while Danjuma's ambition wasn't as grand as becoming ruler of the world, he was intent on reuniting Malika with Dubabi and ruling over the reunified nation. After he gained control of the palace, he would be on his way to making that vision a reality.

He gave the order to attack. His men rushed across the border in a parade of vehicles as they headed for the outpost Colonel Jaheem had set up. They were on the men inside the trailer quickly, although not before they had sounded the alarm.

After dealing with the two guards of the outpost, Danjuma's rebels broke out in laughter as they neared the road leading to the palace. Three teams of four men had been sent out by the palace to respond to the alarm. When they caught sight of the horde of rebels coming at them, they spun their vehicles around and headed back to the main gate that was built into the wall erected around the rim. Had they elected to go head-to-head with such superior numbers, the guards would have died. Far better to hide behind the protection of the wall until help arrived from the army base.

When the truck carrying the Katyusha rocket launcher was in position and ready to fire. Danjuma put a radio to his mouth and gave the order. He decided to use both rockets at once. The main gate was impressive and had been made to withstand an assault by a tank. He had to make certain that it came down.

There was a loud BOOM as a rocket launched. Its aim was true. The rocket impacted the gate, blowing it inward, where it hung from one of its massive iron hinges. As for the second rocket, it was still in the launcher and was hissing and emitting smoke. It blew up without warning, destroying the truck beneath it. Shrapnel sliced through a dozen nearby men causing numerous injuries, all of which were life threatening. The four men nearest the truck had died instantly.

Danjuma cursed the luck before ordering his remaining men to attack. They still outnumbered the guards and soldiers inside the palace. And with Walker in control, the order to surrender would be given soon. The fight would be brief, the general dead, and the day would end with Isaiah Danjuma as ruler of Malika.

Danjuma's rebels were at the rim and rushing through the open gate when he felt the ground beneath his feet tremble.

The first of Soulless's bombs had just gone off.

COLONEL JAHEEM'S PHONE WAS RINGING INCESSANTLY. It would go to voicemail, then ring again. Tanner removed the device from the dead man's pocket and listened to the message left behind. Despite his brief study of the language he couldn't comprehend the message, as it was spoken in the native language of Malika. However, he had recognized the urgent tone and knew that there was trouble.

On a whim, Tanner used Jaheem's phone to take a photo of the general. The assassin, Soulless, had been hired to kill the dictator. Tanner didn't want there to be any dispute over who had actually killed the man. Afterward, he found the switch on the side of the chair that controlled the motor and cut it off. He moved the switch again and sent the chair moving back to its original position. After dragging Victor's corpse clear of the marble platform, Tanner hit the switch a final time. The chair swiveled until its back was facing the room. The rear of the chair had shelves attached, and there were books in them. The section blended into the bookcase surrounding it, and the general's body was out of view.

"Why did you do that?" Palmer asked.

"If the guards can't find his body, they won't be certain that he's dead. It could buy us time to escape if we need it."

He and Palmer left the general's private quarters with their guns at the ready. The instant they opened the thick outer door they heard the alarm blaring.

A man with deep blue eyes and a beard rushed toward them. He was a palace guard they both knew. Tanner had expected to see other men following and for he and Palmer to be their target, but no, the man ignored them and ran past.

Tanner shouted to him. "Cole, what's going on?"

Cole answered over his shoulder while still running. "We're being attacked by the rebels! And they just took down the main gate!" After shouting those words, Cole disappeared around a corner, headed for the armory.

"Shit. Talk about bad timing," Palmer said.

"Not bad for us," Tanner said. "We can leave while everyone else is distracted. While they're fighting the rebels at the eastern rim, we'll make our way beyond the western rim, then move south to the pickup point."

Palmer gripped Tanner's arm. "Are you really going to give me the money you promised?"

Tanner stared at him. "I will. That wasn't a lie."

Palmer grinned. "Let's get the hell out of—" Palmer's next word was cut short as he stopped talking abruptly. A thunderous sound had filled the air, while at the same time the ground trembled violently.

"Earthquake?" Palmer said.

Tanner wondered the same thing. Earthquakes weren't unknown to the region, but they were mild in intensity. The sound and shaking ceased, only to be replaced by an even louder roar. The palace trembled again as the eastern portion of it collapsed.

DANJUMA FELT THE GROUND TREMBLE BENEATH HIS feet and had also come to the conclusion that it must be an earthquake. A smile lit his face. It was an omen, a portent of the victory to come, and the signaling of a new day dawning for Malika.

At the gate, his rebels had overwhelmed the guards they'd encountered. They were suffering casualties, but that was to be expected. The "quake" subsided as quickly as it began. It hadn't been an earthquake, the shaking had been caused by a powerful explosive. The results of that explosion revealed themselves a moment later.

Danjuma looked on in dismay as the eastern side of the rim crumpled inward. The ground beneath it had collapsed and everything above it came crashing down. That included the main gate and ninety-five percent of the rebels. One moment the land was there, and seconds later it had collapsed into the basin, then down into the depths of the earth, burying Danjuma's men, the palace's soldiers and guards, and unknown tons of rock and soil.

Danjuma ordered his driver to take them near the edge. Once there, he looked down into the cloud of dust and could see little. A gap appeared in the swirl of haze and he could make out the palace. A section of it was missing and he could see inside rooms. There was a man hanging over the edge and holding on to what looked like a pipe. He lost his grip and screamed as he plummeted into the pit below. Then the ground shook again, and the western side of the rim collapsed.

Soulless's second bomb had detonated.

~

SOULLESS WAS UP AT THE LAKE WHEN THE BLASTS occurred. He felt the ground shudder beneath his feet even though he was miles away from the site of the detonations.

He was sure that General Kwami was either dead or soon to be so. All that remained for Soulless was to make certain that he couldn't be identified.

The platinum mine drew its water from the lake. This had been accomplished by erecting a small dam. Pipes ran from the dam and down to the buildings on the site. In essence, the lake was used like a water tower. The damn had been a clever idea and had negated the massive expense of continually trucking water in, or of the monumental task of running water pipes from the nearest town. Soulless intended to turn it into a weapon that would make sure that anyone who could identify him was dead.

Perhaps it was overkill. He hadn't spoken to the men who loaded and drove the haul trucks. And yet, he had eaten in the mess hall with them and had been seen by them. On the off chance that the bodies of the miners killed in the cave-ins were recovered, he couldn't allow Frank Brockton, the name he was using, to be the only man missing. By blowing up the dam and flooding the pit, he would not only wipcout the drivers and workers at the quarry by drowning them, he'd also wash away the bodies of the miners, including anyone who survived the cave-ins. The deluge would enter the mine and carry the bodies to new depths created by the blasts. Frank Brockton would be considered one more casualty and not a suspect.

Soulless went to work placing the sixth bomb as close to the dam as he could get it. When the trucks returned to take another load of rock, he'd set the timer and leave the area. Soulless checked his watch, the bomb he'd placed beneath the palace was soon to go off. Everything was going just as he planned. He was blissfully unaware that he had failed to kill his target.

20

THE POWER OF FATE

THE SECOND BOMB HAD KNOCKED TANNER AND Palmer off their feet. The floor beneath them became slanted as another section of the sprawling palace disappeared into the earth. That was followed by the western rim collapsing in a landslide.

"Those are bombs, not an earthquake," Tanner said in an assured tone, as he helped Palmer to stand. He was just as certain that he knew who was behind the bombs—Soulless.

The assassin was known for using a sledgehammer to kill a gnat. Using bombs to cause the collapse of an area just to assassinate one man would fit his previous behavior.

"Who's bombing us?" Palmer asked.

Tanner began walking. He was still headed west. "We have to get out of here as soon as we can."

"Holy Mother of God," Palmer said in a hushed whisper. He and Tanner had just rounded a corner in a corridor. The corridor ended ahead of them. It ended because it was no longer there. Forty feet away was an abyss with dust swirling above it. Beyond that, the evenly carved wall of the western rim was gone, along with the road built into it. The old wall had looked like a series of steps. In its place was a pile of rubble that had been the rim wall and a good portion of the land behind it.

"If the same thing happened to the other road we're trapped down here," Palmer said. "I guess we'll have to climb out."

Palmer was right, they would have to climb out, that is, if they had the time. The palace was only partially destroyed. That meant that Soulless wasn't done with them yet. They had to get out of the palace and beyond the rim as quickly as possible.

Tanner began running. "C'mon Palmer. We're headed to the northern wing."

Palmer tore his gaze away from the devastation and ran to catch up with Tanner. "Where are you going?"

"To the stables," Tanner said.

DANJUMA HAD BEEN STANDING TOO NEAR TO THE edge of the eastern rim when the western rim collapsed. The tremor created made him lose his balance and he went over the side. His hands clutched at loose rock in a desperate attempt to keep himself from sliding down into a hole that was too deep to discern its bottom. When he was thirty feet down, his left hand grabbed onto a piece of stone that was jutting out of the hill. The stone didn't move under his weight and his descent into the pit was halted. If he remained still, he might have a chance to inch his way back up to solid ground.

As his terror subsided, relief mixed with pain as Danjuma became aware that he had injured his right knee. He looked down to see that he had scraped it so badly that he could see bone. Bending the leg was agony, but it did bend. He pushed the pain aside and attempted to move upward. With his damaged knee, the task was next to impossible.

"Mr. Danjuma. Are you all right?"

Danjuma looked up. At first, he saw nothing but the dust still swirling around him, but then a face appeared. It was his driver, a young man who was the son of one of his best fighters. After his father had died in the recent war to gain control of Dubabi, Danjuma had taken the boy under his wing.

"Help me climb up, Yosef."

The face disappeared. Danjuma called to him but

got no response. He was beginning to wonder if the boy had abandoned him when one end of a rope landed beside him.

"Tie that around you and I'll use the car to pull you up."

"Yes. Good thinking, Yosef, but pull me up very slowly."

"Yes sir, I will."

Danjuma carefully secured the rope around him and beneath his arms then lay on his back to protect his damaged knee. True to his word, young Yosef backed the car up ever so slowly. As he neared the top, Danjuma began laughing. He had once again cheated death—or so he thought.

The bomb Soulless had planted outside the general's escape tunnel detonated. Along with the damage already done to the palace, the third explosion was the final straw. Down below, what remained of the palace was swallowed by the massive chasm that had opened up. The honeycomb of underground tunnels collapsed, and their weight combined with that of the palace buckled the stratums below and took it all deeper into the earth.

The entire rim, or what was left of it, shifted yet again, and expanded its edges back farther. The surface that Danjuma was lying on seemed to disappear beneath him for an instant, but then he slammed back down onto it as rocks rained down on him. The rope around him had grown slack, causing him to slide downward again. As before, the piece of stone jutting out halted his slide. Unfortunately, instead of his hand finding purchase, it was Danjuma's crotch that slammed into the rock.

He lay there panting, the fresh pain in his crushed testicles eclipsing that of his knee. His eyes had been clenched shut, but he opened them when he heard the sound of a horn.

The ground that had been supporting the vehicle Yosef was using to pull Danjuma up had crumbled. The sudden jolt forward had thrown Yosef against the steering wheel and his face had hit the horn with enough force to render him senseless. Yosef was fortunate. He would not be awake and aware to experience the horror of what was to happen. He would die without knowing.

Danjuma was not as blessed. He was acutely aware of the vehicle sliding down the steep hill toward him. As it grew nearer, he screamed. The vehicle hit Danjuma, killing him, and sending his body tumbling down into what could only be described as a bottomless pit

A woman known as a witch had told Danjuma and three of his friends their fortunes when he was a boy. He had been told that he would die in his middle years after being struck by a vehicle. Danjuma hadn't taken it seriously at all. Perhaps he should have. That prophecy had now proven to be true.

He had not died alone. Soulless's bombs killed hundreds, the general's protectors and the invading rebels alike. Only a handful remained alive, among them was a man named Tanner.

WATER IN THE HOLE

Tanner had saddled one of the general's horses while Palmer mounted the other one. Tanner had reasoned that the animals would navigate the shifting rocks of the collapsed rim walls better and faster than he and Palmer could ever do on foot.

Palmer hadn't ridden a horse in years but agreed that the animals were their best bet. They had traveled a third of the way up the hill with little difficulty when the third bomb detonated and devastated the land behind them.

Tanner felt the horse drop away underneath him as the ground beneath the horse did the same. His backside found the saddle again as the horse's hooves once more made contact with the disintegrating ground. The animal was having a terrible time with his footing and was sliding backwards toward nothing. Not only were the stables gone, but so was the ground that they had been built upon. A look back disclosed that Palmer's horse was having the same problem, it also revealed a blackness as stygian as death.

Tanner was about to yell to Palmer to jump out of his saddle when his horse halted its backwards slide. Palmer's horse did the same a moment later and the beasts resumed the climb upwards.

"Don't try to guide your horse," Tanner told Palmer. "If there's a way up this hill they'll find it."

"If?" Palmer said.

Tanner didn't answer. He didn't need to. Palmer could see for himself how perilous their situation was.

The ascent was steep and harrowing. For every five steps the horses took forward, they slid three or four steps back, as loose stone covered every surface. Rocks and clumps of dirt from higher up were also bouncing down the hill. A small rock hit Tanner on the arm and he batted away another one that had been headed for his face. The horses were bothered by them too, but their thick hides could withstand it better.

As precarious as the situation was, they were far better staying on the horses. Proof of that came every few seconds. One after another, the surviving men who were climbing on their own would lose their footing and slide into oblivion. Their screams and mewls of whimpering only added to the desperation of the others who would eventually share their fate.

Tanner looked back at Palmer. The man had a death grip on the reins and his face was set in a rictus of terror. Tanner couldn't blame him; the odds were not good on them making it to the top. Still, there was nothing to be done about it. Their fate was intertwined with that of the horses they rode. If the beasts were up to the task, they would live, if not, death would claim them.

Again, the horses lost traction and began sliding back the way they had come. Most of the progress made was lost by the time the animals were able to stop and go forward again.

Tanner felt fearful but not panicked. He had come close to dying at sixteen when his entire family was slaughtered in a massacre. He had considered every blessed day after that as a bonus. And as a master assassin, he knew that when death came for you there was nothing to stop it.

He was also a Tanner. A man trained to overcome incredible odds. Along with the fear he felt confidence in his own survival. He had cheated death before, had survived where others had perished. It would not shock him to do so once again.

After an hour and twenty-three minutes the horses' unending efforts were paying off and they were nearing the top. Tanner heard Palmer cry out in pain and turned to see him looking dazed and with blood seeping from a cut on his forehead. A loose stone, a large one, had bounced past Tanner and struck Palmer.

"Palmer! Don't pass out. Palmer! Hold on!"

Palmer looked back at him with unfocused eyes but nodded.

"Hold on. We're almost there."

Almost turned out to take another four minutes as the horses had great difficulty navigating the final fifty meters. That was where the walls surrounding the rim were, after having crumbled. By then, it was all Palmer could do to maintain his grip on the reigns. Tanner's horse crested the hill first. He dismounted and rushed to assist Palmer. The man looked as if he were a drunk who had been forced to stay awake for days. There was no doubt that he had a concussion. Tanner fought the urge to relax his guard and guided Palmer's horse farther away from the edge. It would be tragic to have fought their way up the steep hill only to have the ground beneath them give way again. Finally, when he felt they were secure. Tanner relaxed.

"You're safe," Tanner said to Palmer, and watched as the last shred of consciousness fled the man.

Tanner caught him as he slid off the saddle and lowered him to the ground.

There were four survivors of the destruction of the palace—two horses and two men.

Tanner lifted Palmer up and carried him to the shade of a tree. He would come back for him after making contact with the extraction team.

He straddled the horse again and headed off in the direction of the train tracks. As he rode, he was looking forward to returning home.

THE FOUR HAUL TRUCKS HAD RETURNED TO THE MINE during the time Tanner was making his harrowing escape up the steep hillside above the cavity that had been created by the bombs. Soulless watched one of the drivers get out and look inside the guard shack. The man must have been wondering where the security guards had gone.

After getting back inside his huge vehicle, the man drove his truck down to the area at the bottom of the pit where a new load of rock awaited him. The trucks moved slowly even though they were empty. From Soulless's position up at the lake, they looked like four lumbering beasts as they wound their way deeper into the pit along the road carved from the rock. He estimated how much time they would need to reach the bottom and programmed his sixth and final bomb. With that done, Soulless straddled his motorcycle. He was headed to a spot higher up that overlooked the lake and the mine. He wanted to see what would happen once the dam gave way. He figured it would be quite a show.

As he reached the hill and settled in, he realized that the fourth bomb he'd left inside the mine would actually be the last to explode. He had set it to go off late. If anyone survived at the palace, the fourth bomb would remedy that.

The Irish woman, Gwen, had told him that the fourth bomb was pure overkill and that the first three "packages" would be enough to destroy the palace, and then some. Soulless used four bombs anyway. He figured, what would be the harm?

He heard a muffled sound and felt the ground tremble as the fifth bomb went off down inside the mine. It was now time for the sixth bomb to detonate.

The haul trucks had been lining up to be filled when the dam was destroyed in a spectacular explosion that sent concrete, dirt, and several trees flying through the air. The bomb had destroyed the dam and removed a wide section of the basin that had been enclosing the lake water. Millions of gallons began cascading down the hillside at a furious rate.

Soulless could see the men in the pit below pointing up at the massive flow. They had yet to comprehend that their lives were in danger. That realization came minutes later as the lake water reached them and lapped at their feet.

The haul truck drivers and the men in charge of loading piled into two pickup trucks that were used to ferry people back and forth between the mine and the nearby plant that processed the ore. Soulless frowned at the sight. He hadn't remembered the pickup trucks. It was possible that the drivers might get away.

He needn't have worried. On a normal road, the men would have made good progress and reached a higher elevation quickly. The roughhewn road leading out of the pit was navigable but not efficient. It wound its way up the vast pit but in a fashion that only allowed vehicles to gradually rise in elevation. It proved to be too slow.

The pickup trucks were flirting with death as they sped along a track that had no guardrails and was littered with bumps and dips. As they were forced to slow, in order to make dozens of turns to gain progress, the lake water was rising steadily. Some of the water was draining down into the mine as Soulless had intended, but at a rate that was a fraction of the inflow.

The pickup trucks still had five levels of the road

to deal with when the water reached the height of their hoods. The liquid also blocked the view of the road ahead of them. Soulless couldn't be sure if the drivers had gone off the road or whether the water had lifted the trucks up, but they began to float along like corks.

As the water level rose higher, Soulless thought the pit might overflow. That possibility was denied as the mine opening expanded due to the pressure of the inflowing water.

As the water poured with renewed volume down the mineshaft to fill numerous caverns and tunnels, a whirlpool formed on the surface. The pickup trucks were sucked into the center of it, along with the men inside them. One of the men managed to jump out of his truck, to try to swim away. The others foolishly did the same.

The swirling water was moving too swiftly for them to escape. Within minutes the men were dead. They had been caught between the pickup trucks as they slammed against each other repeatedly, it added a dash of red to the brown water.

Soulless would have liked to stay and watch the lake drain completely, but he realized that would be stupid and increase his chances of being seen. Besides, he had a train to catch.

Soulless watched the vortex swirl for a few seconds longer before getting on the motorcycle and speeding down the hill. If General Kwami hadn't been blown up or crushed inside his escape tunnel, there was a chance he might drown.

Everyone and anyone who could possibly identify him was dead or dying. It was time to get out of the country and enjoy time off for a job well done.

22

STANDOFF

TANNER REACHED THE RAILROAD TRACKS AND entered the small stand of trees that were nearby. He found the marker, uncovered the signal beacon, and activated it. Afterward, he had to wait for someone to respond. Lawson had told him that a helicopter would be picking him up. That same chopper could fly back toward the palace—where the palace had once been—and he could get Palmer.

An unexpected sight off in the distance mystified Tanner as he stood among the trees. In the east, in the area where the platinum mine was located, he saw a geyser of water shoot into the air. It reached a height of over two hundred feet.

The rapid displacement of air in the mine shafts and caverns sent compressed air out through an opening in an abandoned mine in the same area.

That air was followed by a blast of water that could be seen for miles.

As the geyser subsided, Tanner's gaze lowered. Light glinted off something a few miles away. It was a train. Then the sound of a motor approaching could be heard. Tanner thought it might be the helicopter he was expecting and wondered how they had gotten to him so quickly. But no, it wasn't anything in the air. It was a motorcycle.

SOULLESS WAS RIDING ALONG PARALLEL TO THE railroad tracks. He was on the opposite side of them from where Tanner was. He didn't realize the train was behind him until he had shut off his engine and taken off his helmet. When he saw that the train was approaching, he was glad he wouldn't need to wait for long.

He had considered riding away on the motorcycle, but it was stolen and low on gas. He had pressed his luck by using it as long as he had anyway. By hiding aboard the freight train, he could ride it all the way down to South Africa. From there, he would make his way west and eventually end up in the Caribbean.

An image of the Irish woman flashed across the screen of his mind. It surprised him that he would be thinking of her. Somehow, she had left an impression on him. He wished that he were meeting her in the islands.

The train was growing nearer. He would ride alongside it while on the motorcycle then take hold of a grab bar to pull himself onto the train. The lumbering freight train had over twenty cars and was moving at less than thirty miles an hour. Before that happened, he needed to relieve his bladder. He unzipped his fly, did his business, and had just pulled the zipper back up when he sensed that he was no longer alone.

Soulless spun around and found a man staring at him from across the railroad tracks. There was something familiar about the face, but it was the eyes that identified him. And what eyes the man had. They were eyes that Soulless had seen on a wanted poster once, and in a sketch when a reward had been offered for the man. Neither had done that intense gaze justice.

Recognition spawned a realization. There was only one reason the man would be in the area. It was the same reason that Soulless had traveled so far to be there. He had come to Africa to kill General Kwami.

A sick feeling began to form in the pit of Soulless's stomach as the notion that he could have failed entered his mind. Reason denied that there was a cause for it. *He* had killed the general, not the man standing before him. It was not possible.

Soulless took in a deep breath, released it slowly, and forced himself to smile as he took a step closer to the tracks.

"Hello, Tanner. They call me Soulless."

TANNER HADN'T NEEDED SOULLESS TO CONFIRM HIS identity; somehow, he had known who it was he was looking at. They were about the same height, but Soulless was younger by a decade or more. Where his eyes drew attention to him and were memorable, Soulless was the opposite. He was neither handsome nor plain and could blend into most crowds. That was the physical aspect of the man. His aura was another matter. It was what had made Tanner so certain that the man with the motorcycle was a killer. Soulless radiated a quiet menace. Tanner was certain that most people wouldn't sense it, but he did. The cold smile the man sent him as he introduced himself did nothing to alleviate the feeling of danger.

He sent his fellow assassin a nod and asked the obvious question. "You're here to kill the general?"

"I have killed the general. His body is buried under tons of rubble. If you're here, that means you were hired to kill him too. My bombs beat you to it."

"I thought those bombs were your work. It fits your reputation."

Tanner's calm response to being told that another man had killed the target he was after seemed to surprise Soulless. But then he squared his shoulders and wore a smirk.

"You have a reputation for never failing to kill a target. I guess that's over now."

Tanner shook his head. "My reputation is intact."

"Meaning?"

"I killed General Kwami before the bombs went off."

Soulless heard Tanner's words and felt the sick feeling in the pit of his stomach return. Hadn't his bombs killed General Kwami? Yes! There was no way for that not to be the case. The man standing before him was formidable and considered to be the greatest assassin of all time, but he was a man and he had failed. The bastard was intending to take credit for his work. Anger was an emotion seldom felt by Soulless, but it was growing inside him along with a sense of injustice. How dare the man try to claim his kill as his own.

"You're lying, Tanner. If you'd been anywhere near the general, you would be dead along with him. You were the best at one time, but everyone fails. I won't let you take credit for one of my kills."

"I'm going to reach into my pocket for a cell phone," Tanner said. "Don't get trigger happy."

Soulless remained silent. He watched as Tanner removed a cell phone from the inside pocket of the suit jacket he wore.

A soft rumble carried on the air as the train grew closer. Soulless risked a glance to his right and estimated that the train would pass by in less than a minute. It was how much time he had to kill Tanner. The man had seen his face. He could not be allowed to live.

Tanner pressed buttons on the phone. As he did so, Soulless saw that his gaze never left him for more than a fraction of a second. The man was wary, as he should be. It wouldn't matter. Soulless was confident that he would be faster on the draw than Tanner. He had never met anyone who was faster than he was.

Tanner held up the phone in his left hand as the horn on the train announced its approach. The engineer driving it must have seen them standing on opposite sides of the tracks. Soulless gave the train a quick glance again. When it grew closer and distracted Tanner, that's when he would make his move.

"Look at the picture on the phone," Tanner said.

Soulless did so. He did it so briefly that he took in little more than an impression of what the photo revealed. It was enough to make him forego caution, take his eyes off Tanner, and stare at the image on the screen. It displayed a photo of General Mohamed Kwami, leader of Malika, lying dead in a chair. He'd been the victim of a gunshot wound to the head.

No! No! No! screamed a voice inside Soulless. All his work, all the planning, all his time spent in that dark and filthy mine had been for nothing. And it was Tanner's fault.

The train blew its horn again. Soulless saw Tanner's eyes flick left to look at the approaching locomotive. It was time for the bastard to die.

THE TRAIN ENGINEER WAS BLOWING HIS HORN AGAIN as the train barreled toward the two men near the tracks.

Soulless drew his gun in a blur of motion as Tanner did the same. Both men were aiming at each other's head as they pulled their triggers.

23

UNINTENDED CONSEQUENCES

TANNER WAS EXPECTING IT WHEN SOULLESS DREW HIS weapon, he had not been anticipating the man to be so fast.

As Tanner was pulling on the trigger, the ground beneath his feet rose up with tremendous force and sent him falling backwards. The round he'd fired went into the air and missed its intended target.

Soulless had likewise missed.

Stunned, and wondering what had happened, Tanner sat up to see that a section of the ground and the railroad tracks bulged as if pushed upwards. They were curved and leaning toward Soulless's side of the tracks.

He made it to his feet as Soulless did the same on the other side. A discordant squeal began as the train engineer tried to bring the locomotive to a halt.

Soulless was staring at the tracks and looking as stunned as Tanner. His expression turned into one of concern as he realized the train would derail.

After glancing toward Tanner, he turned and began sprinting to put distance between himself and the tracks. If he had run at twice the speed, he would have been too slow. The screeching of the train's brakes ceased as the multi-ton beast hit the mangled section of track and went airborne. The locomotive hit a height of eleven feet before smashing into the ground. The railroad cars behind it were filled with sand. They too tipped onto their sides. Their momentum along with the sheer massive weight of their cargo ensured that they remained moving.

Tanner saw Soulless look over his shoulder as the train bore down on him. There was no panic on the man's face, just a grim expression. Tanner's last glimpse of Soulless was a view of the man trying to dive out of the path of the train. It was a weak attempt that carried him forward rather than to the side. A moment later the train passed over the spot where Soulless had been. The weight of the train must have squashed him like a bug being hit by a brick.

THE TRAIN DERAILMENT HAD BEEN CAUSED BY THE fourth bomb that Soulless had placed beneath the palace. With the spectacle and the thunderous sound of the draining lake to distract him, Soulless had just assumed that the fourth of his six bombs would go off as planned. He was mistaken. Water from the lake had reached the bomb and played havoc with its electronic timer.

The device was capable of floating. It drifted along on a stream of water inside a narrow cavern that had taken it in a southwesterly direction. Like Soulless, it arrived at the railroad tracks. The red digits on its timer had counted down the minutes until it exploded with devastating consequences beneath the railroad tracks.

TANNER HAD NO IDEA WHAT HAD CAUSED THE GROUND to rise up the way it did. During the moment the bomb went off underground, the train's horn had drowned out the sound of it. He rushed to the front of the train to see if there were any survivors. Sand was everywhere as many of the cars had tipped over, and he had to make his way across it to reach the engine.

He found two men who'd died from injuries

caused by the derailment. They were the train's conductor and engineer.

The sixth train car was over the spot where he'd last seen Soulless. Given what had happened to him, Tanner guessed that he had been smeared across a wide section of ground. What was left of him was covered up by the sand.

A familiar sound overhead caught his attention. It was a helicopter. His ride out of the country had arrived. The pilot and copilot were suitably agog at the scene they landed near. Their astonishment increased when Tanner directed them toward the site where there had once been a complex and the home of the country's dictator. The dust had finally settled, but even from the air there seemed to be no bottom to the abyss that Soulless had created.

Palmer was still unconscious when the copilot helped Tanner to get him onboard. As they flew away, in the distance was a convoy of army vehicles. Tanner wondered why their response had been so delayed, but he assumed that it had been arranged so Walker, who had sought to kill the general, could gain control of the country.

Sheep needed a shepherd. Lawson would team up with the general's son to provide one or someone else would fill the vacuum. Such things didn't interest Tanner. He was hired to do a job and did it. The general was dead. Now, it was time to go home.

24

PHOENIX

THE SPECTACULAR DEMISE OF THE MALIKAN DICTATOR General Kwami made news worldwide. Tanner called Sara as soon as he was able to and let her know that he was all right. As they spoke, she went online to look at images of the site where the palace had been. Sara saw aerial photographs showing what the compound had looked like before and after the bombs went off.

"Oh my God! You were there when *that* happened?"

"Yes. It was… interesting. I'll tell you all about it when I get home."

"How soon will that be?"

"Probably the day after tomorrow. There's a lot of travel involved, and I have an errand I still have to see to."

PALMER HAD BEEN PLACED INSIDE A HOSPITAL IN South Africa under an assumed name, thanks to Thomas Lawson's connections. He was sitting up in bed with his head wrapped in a bandage. Palmer had suffered a serious concussion and needed to rest.

Tanner handed him an envelope as he took a seat near the bed.

"What's this?"

"Open it and see."

Palmer did so. He found that the envelope contained five-thousand euros and an index card with alphanumeric codes written on it, along with a phone number.

"The cash is just traveling money. The numbers written on that card belong to the bank account your real money is in."

Palmer smiled. "You really paid me?"

Tanner handed him a phone. "Call that number and follow the directions you hear. It's all automated."

Palmer made the call. He reacted to instructions given to him by an electronic voice by hitting the keys on the phone that corresponded to the numbers and letters on the card. He was informed that he had a balance of one million pounds.

"Bloody hell. I'm rich."

"Not for long. I'm sure your wife's medical care will eat up a chunk of that."

Palmer sniffled. "I can help her now. She's going to be okay."

Tanner stood. "I have a flight to catch."

"Hey, mate. What's your real name? I'm betting it's not Foxx."

"You can call me Tanner."

Palmer held up the card with the bank account info on it.

"Look me up if you ever need help. I owe you one."

Tanner sent him a nod and left the room. He was eager to return home.

THE SITE OF THE FREAK TRAIN DERAILMENT HAD BEEN less noteworthy than it normally would have been due to the destruction of the palace and the mayhem at the mine. Those incidents had also demanded the attention of emergency crews. By the time cleanup began along the railroad tracks, over thirty hours had passed. The bodies of the engineer and conductor had been recovered the day before.

A four-man night crew was assigned to do the work and were intent on righting the train cars that lay on their sides. A special crane was erected in order to accomplish that.

When they were lifting the sixth freight car, they discovered that there was a fissure in the road beneath it. The crack covered over twenty feet and was three feet wide at its middle. How far down it went was anyone's guess. The work crew became aware that more than sand had gone inside the hole when the derailment occurred. There was also a man down in there. Someone was calling to them from inside the fissure.

Astonishment gave way to action. The crew had a fifty-foot length of rope; they used it to help pull the man out of the hole. Remarkably, other than minor cuts and bruises and the need for hydration, the man appeared to be well.

SOULLESS SUCKED DOWN THE BOTTLE OF WATER ONE of his rescuers had given him. He repaid the man's kindness by shooting him in the back of the head. The other three men died next. They had seen his face.

Tanner had also seen his face, knew what he looked like, and had had the audacity to point his weapon at him. He had also cheated Soulless by robbing him of the chance to assassinate the general.

The man had to die.

Soulless searched the dead men until he found the keys that belonged to a red pickup truck. He sat in the truck and took something out of his pocket. It was the gold coin that he had intended to represent his killing of the general.

Since he couldn't place it in the general's mouth, he'd intended to send it and a letter to a reporter and claim responsibility for Kwami's death. He could no longer do that.

Soulless squeezed the coin in his hand in a tight grip. He'd hold onto it. Someday he would shove it into Tanner's mouth, right between his dead and lifeless lips.

Once he had the truck in motion, Soulless headed south.

He'd run into Tanner again someday. He would make a point of it.

And on that day, Tanner would die.

Soulless drove on, knowing he was second-best. The fact of it ate away at his dark soul.

TANNER RETURNS!

TO SERVE AND PROTECT - TANNER 39 -
AVAILABLE FOR PRE-ORDER - ON SALE
NOVEMBER 17th

AFTERWORD

Thank you,

REMINGTON KANE

The TANNER Series in order

MISSING - A Tanner Novel - Book 37

CONTENDER - A Tanner Novel - Book 38

TO SERVE AND PROTECT - A Tanner Novel - Book 39

STALKING HORSE - A Tanner Novel - Book 40

THE EVIL OF TWO LESSERS - A Tanner Novel - Book 41

SINS OF THE FATHER AND MOTHER - A Tanner Novel - Book 42

SOULLESS - A Tanner Novel - Book 43

The Young Guns Series in order

YOUNG GUNS

YOUNG GUNS 2 - SMOKE & MIRRORS

YOUNG GUNS 3 - BEYOND LIMITS

YOUNG GUNS 4 - RYKER'S RAIDERS

YOUNG GUNS 5 - ULTIMATE TRAINING

YOUNG GUNS 6 - CONTRACT TO KILL

YOUNG GUNS 7 - FIRST LOVE

YOUNG GUNS 8 - THE END OF THE BEGINNING

A Tanner Series in order

TANNER: YEAR ONE

TANNER: YEAR TWO

TANNER: YEAR THREE

TANNER: YEAR FOUR

TANNER: YEAR FIVE

The TAKEN! Series in order

TAKEN! - LOVE CONQUERS ALL - Book 1

TAKEN! - SECRETS & LIES - Book 2

TAKEN! - STALKER - Book 3

TAKEN! - BREAKOUT! - Book 4

TAKEN! - THE THIRTY-NINE - Book 5

TAKEN! - KIDNAPPING THE DEVIL - Book 6

TAKEN! - HIT SQUAD - Book 7

TAKEN! - MASQUERADE - Book 8

TAKEN! - SERIOUS BUSINESS - Book 9

TAKEN! - THE COUPLE THAT SLAYS TOGETHER - Book 10

TAKEN! - PUT ASUNDER - Book 11

TAKEN! - LIKE BOND, ONLY BETTER - Book 12

TAKEN! - MEDIEVAL - Book 13

TAKEN! - RISEN! - Book 14

TAKEN! - VACATION - Book 15

TAKEN! - MICHAEL - Book 16

TAKEN! - BEDEVILED - Book 17

TAKEN! - INTENTIONAL ACTS OF VIOLENCE - Book 18

TAKEN! - THE KING OF KILLERS – Book 19

TAKEN! - NO MORE MR. NICE GUY - Book 20 & the Series Finale

The MR. WHITE Series

PAST IMPERFECT - MR. WHITE - Book 1

HUNTED - MR. WHITE - Book 2

The BLUE STEELE Series in order

BLUE STEELE - BOUNTY HUNTER- Book 1

BLUE STEELE - BROKEN- Book 2

BLUE STEELE - VENGEANCE- Book 3

BLUE STEELE - THAT WHICH DOESN'T KILL ME- Book 4

BLUE STEELE - ON THE HUNT- Book 5

BLUE STEELE - PAST SINS - Book 6

BLUE STEELE - DADDY'S GIRL - Book 7 & the Series Finale

The CALIBER DETECTIVE AGENCY Series in order

CALIBER DETECTIVE AGENCY - GENERATIONS- Book 1

CALIBER DETECTIVE AGENCY - TEMPTATION-
Book 2

CALIBER DETECTIVE AGENCY - A RANSOM PAID
IN BLOOD- Book 3

CALIBER DETECTIVE AGENCY - MISSING- Book 4

CALIBER DETECTIVE AGENCY - DECEPTION-
Book 5

CALIBER DETECTIVE AGENCY - CRUCIBLE- Book 6

CALIBER DETECTIVE AGENCY – LEGENDARY –
Book 7

CALIBER DETECTIVE AGENCY – WE ARE
GATHERED HERE TODAY - Book 8

CALIBER DETECTIVE AGENCY - MEANS, MOTIVE,
and OPPORTUNITY - Book 9 & the Series Finale

THE TAKEN!/TANNER Series in order

THE CONTRACT: KILL JESSICA WHITE -
Taken!/Tanner - Book 1

UNFINISHED BUSINESS – Taken!/Tanner – Book 2

THE ABDUCTION OF THOMAS LAWSON -
Taken!/Tanner – Book 3

PREDATOR - Taken!/Tanner - Book 4

DETECTIVE PIERCE Series in order

MONSTERS - A Detective Pierce Novel - Book 1

DEMONS - A Detective Pierce Novel - Book 2

ANGELS - A Detective Pierce Novel - Book 3

THE OCEAN BEACH ISLAND Series in order

THE MANY AND THE ONE - Book 1

SINS & SECOND CHANES - Book 2

DRY ADULTERY, WET AMBITION -Book 3

OF TONGUE AND PEN - Book 4

ALL GOOD THINGS… - Book 5

LITTLE WHITE SINS - Book 6

THE LIGHT OF DARKNESS - Book 7

STERN ISLAND - Book 8 & the Series Finale

THE REVENGE Series in order

JOHNNY REVENGE - The Revenge Series - Book 1

THE APPOINTMENT KILLER - The Revenge Series - Book 2

AN I FOR AN I - The Revenge Series - Book 3

ALSO

THE EFFECT: Reality is changing!

THE FIX-IT MAN: A Tale of True Love and Revenge

DOUBLE OR NOTHING

PARKER & KNIGHT

REDEMPTION: Someone's taken her

DESOLATION LAKE

TIME TRAVEL TALES & OTHER SHORT STORIES

Printed in Great Britain
by Amazon

84763582R00160